SARAH M. ANDERSON WRITING AS

MAGGIE CHASE

HIS
DIAMOND

ISBN-13: 978-1-941097-43-4

Chapter One

Cynthia Hobbs paused in the hall outside the parlor to remove her stained apron and check her reflection in the mirror. One curl had come loose from her bun and she was a little flushed, but considering the temper Sarah was in today, she looked presentable.

Overhead Cynthia heard an ominous *thump*. She shouldn't have left her sister alone with only Doreen to watch over her. Sarah was too strong and too stubborn for any one maid to manage, especially before she'd had her nap.

It took a moment for Cynthia to remember how to smile. She was never to show the strain of caring for Sarah because, for all intents and purposes, the girl didn't exist. The entire town of Brimstone, Texas, believed Cynthia was the vain and spoiled daughter of Gerald Hobbs, owner of the First Macon County Bank. Nothing more and nothing less.

Another *thump* overhead. Cynthia winced. Her father knew this was the time of day when Sarah was most unruly—why was he calling her away from the nursery now?

Only one way to find out. Cynthia squared her shoulders and worked hard for that vapid, spoiled smile. Then she sailed into the parlor as if she had

1

nothing more pressing to do than decide on the color of her next hat. God forbid anyone know that Gerald Hobbs had a daughter who did anything as base as work. "Good afternoon, Father."

She pulled up short when she recognized the other man in the room—a man she knew better than she wanted to. Vincent Brown was the vice president at First Macon and her father's favorite.

He didn't bother standing when she entered the room. But then again, neither did her father.

Oh, it took work to keep the smile on her face and ignore the slight. "You wanted to see me?" she asked, keeping her voice high and light. Untroubled.

Her father's eyes narrowed. Perhaps she should try harder.

"Cynthia. There you are," he began, almost presenting a believable version of a concerned father. "I have some wonderful news to share with you."

Cynthia's stomach twisted. What her father considered *wonderful news* was always a disaster. "Oh?" Her cheeks were beginning to hurt. Smiling was difficult on the best of days in the Hobbs household.

Her father waited for a moment, his gaze cataloging her misplaced curl, her flush. She would hear of her faults later, no doubt. "I offer you my congratulations, my dear."

Cynthia waited a respectable second before being forced to ask, "Why, thank you. But what has prompted such warm feelings?"

Vincent Brown's smile took on a sneer as he hefted his bulk out of the leather chair next to her father's desk. "I must say, Miss Hobbs, you look delectable today."

Delectable. She hadn't heard that one for a long

time. Vincent was fond of compliments that made it sound like he wanted to eat her for dinner. The last time she'd been forced to endure his company, *delicious* had been his word of choice. "Thank you, Mr. Brown." Her smile locked into place, she looked back to her father, without offering her hand to Mr. Brown for a sloppy kiss.

"I have decided that you and Vincent will marry," her father began with no other introduction. "You have a month to plan."

Overhead, another ominous *thump*.

Cynthia did not dare breathe. Not so much as blink. Surely her father had not just said she had to marry Vincent? The man was in his mid-forties if he was a day, and he had a paunch that even now was straining at the buttons on his waistcoat. His hair was thin, his mustache thinner and his eyes were small and piggish.

Piggish and cruel.

"I'm sorry," Cynthia began, launching another smile into the room. "I must've misheard. I…"

Her father's nostrils flared with anger. "Something wrong with your hearing, girl? Vincent has asked for your hand and I've given permission. What else is there to discuss?"

Insolence was not tolerated in this household. But this was too important. "But what about Sarah?"

Her father shuffled some papers. "What about her?" Unsurprisingly, his voice was cold and hard. He was ashamed of Sarah, of her imperfections.

Vincent took another step closer, his gaze fastened on Cynthia's bosom. "Your father has explained the situation with your dear, dear sister. I know that you do your best to care for the poor thing. I have assured him

3

that I will be delighted to have you bring Sarah with you when you join my household. I would hate to break up a pair of sisters."

It was only then that he raised his eyes to hers. Cynthia fought against the shiver racing down her back, but she lost that battle when Vincent swiped a thumb over the corner of his mouth, catching the tip of the digit with his tongue.

"I understand," he went on in a voice that would haunt Cynthia's dreams, "that your sister is mentally deficient but I can assure you I will show her the same favor I will show you." He captured her hand and brought it to his mouth, coating her knuckles in spittle.

"How... kind of you," Cynthia said, unable to do anything about the waver in her voice.

"Then it's settled," her father said.

The dismissal was obvious. Cynthia turned to go, but Vincent still had her hand, damn him. He gave her a quick tug and said, "I'm looking forward to our wedding night," in a quiet voice that was all the more sinister because of it.

She could feel her father's gaze burning into her so, somehow, she managed an innocent blush and said, "As am I," in a tone that might've been believable.

Vincent dropped her hand and turned away. The dismissal was complete. Cynthia curtsied to no one in particular—neither man was paying attention to her—and then backed out of the room.

Overhead, there was a crash and Cynthia knew she should rush up to the third floor and keep her sister from destroying herself and the house, and the maid for good measure. But for a long moment, all she could do was sag against the newel post of the banister.

She was twenty. She should've already married and started a family of her own. But Sarah needed her and her father had never approved of any of the many suitors who had attempted to court Cynthia. Gerald Hobbs controlled the money in this town. No one dared go against him.

How could he mean to marry her to Vincent Brown? How could he do that to Sarah?

How could he do that to *her*?

One month. She had one month to find a way out of this mess and save her sister from a lifetime of sexual abuse at the hands of Vincent Brown.

What was she going to do?

*

"It's not a bad place," Cam Douglas said as he eyed the First Macon County Bank in downtown Brimstone.

In response to this observation, his young partner, Hatfield, turned and spat into the dirt street.

Cam grinned. "Of course, that doesn't make it a good place. Sort of... in between."

Hatfield rolled his eyes.

Cam knew the boy could talk. He'd heard Hat shout warnings at coachmen who'd thought they were going to somehow outshoot Black Cam and Hatfield the Kid.

Those stagecoach drivers tended to wind up with a bullet hole in their arms or legs. Cam never aimed to kill, but he did aim to disable.

"It's not a stagecoach," Cam went on. Just because Hatfield could talk didn't mean he contributed

5

to the conversation. The kid rarely said anything. "We haven't robbed a lot of banks."

Point of fact, they hadn't robbed any. Stagecoaches—those were easy. Pick a good spot to get the drop on the driver, wing the rider with the gun so he couldn't get off a shot, unhitch the horses and make off with the valuables. They were good at stagecoaches. Stagecoaches kept them in whiskey and kept Cam in women.

Banks? Another matter entirely. A man didn't wait for a bank to come to him. He had to go to the bank. Even worse? The Brimstone Jail was right across the street. Winging a rider with a gun was a big difference from shooting a sheriff, accident or not.

Cam scratched at his neck. He'd prefer not to hang over this job, but what the hell. Someone wanted the First Macon County Bank robbed. They had a plan—a damned good plan, Cam knew. Better than anything he could come up with. They just needed the hired muscle to actually pull off the job.

"I don't know," he said, mostly to himself. "Seems risky."

Hatfield spat again, but this time in agreement.

"I mean, if I want to rob a bank, I'll rob a bank," Cam went on, pivoting on his heels and walking away. "I'll do it for myself. For us," he added, mindful that he was not the boss of Hatfield. They were a team. "Not for some shadowy figure that doesn't want his hands dirty."

Hatfield grunted, which was practically the same thing as him shouting in agreement.

"Then you gotta ask yourself *why*," Cam went on. "Why does this man want to rob this bank on that specific date, in that specific way? Yeah, there's the money, but it feels like a setup," he concluded, looking back at the bank.

Hatfield made a sound of warning, but by then it was too late—Cam had collided with someone. "Oof!"

The first thing he thought was *soft*, followed quickly, and strangely, by *purple*.

Mine was the third thing.

He moved without thinking, wrapping his arms around the girl's waist to keep her from falling onto her backside in the middle of the dirty street. He hauled her against him and spun, struggling to keep his balance so he didn't topple them both. That feat of acrobatics brought her breasts in full contact with his chest. He stumbled as something in his brain misfired, repeating *Mine*. He clutched her even tighter and in that moment, there was no hope of finding his balance. He staggered backward, tripping and going down like a sack of bricks, the back of his head bouncing off the boardwalk. The woman landed on top of him with a gasped, "*Oh!*"

His head ached dully, but she was sprawled on top of him, his arms around her waist, her weight pressing down against him. She felt so good there and his body leapt to appreciate her properly.

Yeah, he didn't give a damn about his head.

He got his eyes to focus at the same moment she pushed herself up, her hands flat on his chest. Which drove her hips against his. God, she was going to kill him and he was going to die a happy man.

Then the full impact of her appearance hit him, harder than any boardwalk ever could. Her hat had been knocked aside, revealing a riot of gorgeous blonde curls. His hands had already started tracing a path up her back toward that hair before he got them under control.

But that wasn't the worst part. No, the worst part was her eyes, a pretty light blue that was like the summer sky on a perfect day. She was the most stunning woman he'd ever fallen for.

"Beautiful."

"I beg your pardon?"

Shit, had he said that out loud? He must have hit his head harder than he'd thought. "Apologies, Miss," he said quickly because it was the only thing he could come up with.

She pushed against his chest again and damned if he didn't want to pull her right back down into his arms.

A look of alarm crossed her face. Oh, right. They were lying in the middle of the boardwalk. She was on top of him. People were probably beginning to stare. He sat up, which led to her straddling his lap, her skirts tangling around both their legs.

"My apologies," he said again, forcing himself to let go of her. "I didn't see you there."

Hatfield appeared, grabbing the elbow of the young lady and hoisting her to her feet.

"The fault was mine," the blonde said, adjusting her hat and trying to get her curls tucked up under the brim again. "I was distracted."

Now that she was no longer on top of him, Cam got a good look at her and his mouth fell open. The girl wore a gown of lustrous purple silk so dark it was almost black, cut to show off the sweeping expanse of her bosom without being vulgar. Her hair was swept up, generous curls rioting out from under the brim of her broad hat.

This girl was the loveliest woman he had ever seen and he had seen a lot of lovely women. She was sweet and young and innocent-looking, like she didn't have a care in the world. At the sight of her, something sighed in his chest. True beauty was so rare in his world. He appreciated it all the more when he did see it.

Mine.

He had no claim to this girl, no right to even look at her, much less hold her in his arms. But tell that to his body.

She got her hat fixed and shook out her skirts while Hatfield hauled Cam to his feet. Once he was sure he could stand, he whipped off his hat and held it over his heart. "Ma'am," he said, striving for gentlemanly as he inclined his head. Belatedly, he wished he'd gotten a shave or a bath. He probably looked like, well, like a stagecoach robber.

His greeting was not gentlemanly enough, apparently. The girl's eyes widened for a fraction of the second and Cam had just enough time to hope he was seeing attraction instead of fear when a strange sort of emptiness stole over her face.

Cam didn't like that emptiness.

But he didn't say that. Instead, he said, "Are you all right? That was a rather rough landing."

"Yes, I believe so." She tried to smile but it still looked off. "And you? You took the worst of it, I'm afraid. Thank you for that."

"Nothing any gentleman wouldn't do for a lady," he said. Her not-smile got more real, somehow, drawing him in.

He got a grip on himself before he leaned down to touch her lips with his fingers, or worse his own mouth, in what would be a long, leisurely exploration of lips and tongues. She was clearly a young woman of means and quality and Cam was a wanted man. He had no right to touch her, no right to even think of her.

To keep himself from doing something crazy, he looked around. Her reticule and parasol were on the ground. He bent to retrieve her things, which also gave him the opportunity to study her figure as he straightened. In that dress, she was a vision. But what would she look like out of it?

She cleared her throat. "Thank you," she said when Cam got his eyes back where they belonged— her face. She took her things from him. Even though she was wearing gloves, the blood in his veins began to pound when her fingertips skimmed over the palm of his hand.

Jesus, how was she doing this to him? He was Cam Douglas—Black Cam, the stagecoach robber. And this slip of a woman had reduced him to a babbling idiot.

"Again, my apologies." The parasol was bent at an angle and there was dirt on the hem of her dress. He winced inwardly. It would've been worse if he hadn't been able to take the fall for her, but still. "If there's ever anything I can do to make it up to you, Miss… "

She looked up at him and the emptiness was gone. For the shortest of seconds, her mouth opened and there was something haunted in her eyes and Cam just had time to think *she needs me* before she snapped her mouth shut and straightened her spine.

"That won't be necessary. Good day."

10

Then, with her head held high, she swept past him and Hat. Well. That was that, apparently.

Damn. She hadn't given him her name.

Cam glanced over to see Hatfield smirking at him. "What? She was a beauty."

Hatfield lifted an eyebrow.

"I was being polite. You should try it sometimes."

Hatfield rolled his eyes and began to walk down the boardwalk again.

Right. They weren't here for him to moon over ladies. Cam dusted off his ass and crammed his hat back on his head. He didn't feel a knot on the back, just a sore spot that left him with a little bit of a headache.

"We need more information," Cam said, trying to focus on the job at hand. That didn't stop him from looking back at the girl, though. Head high, shoulders back—she looked soft and inviting but he could see steel in her spine.

A strange sort of *want* settled in his chest. Not straight lust, but something much more powerful than her beauty should've inspired. That pretty miss pulled at him in ways that didn't make a damned bit of sense. All he knew was he wanted to stride right back down the street and pull her into his arms again, and this time he didn't want to let go of her.

"If we knew who wanted the job pulled," he went on, trying to focus, "it'd go a long way toward making me feel better about my place in the world."

She stopped in front of the bank. Cam put his hand on Hatfield's shoulder and watched. The young lady squared her shoulders even more—Cam wouldn't have thought it possible, but she did. She looked... alone. Brimstone was a bustling town and many folks were out doing their daily chores, but that woman stood apart.

She glanced back down the street and their gazes collided. Cam whipped off his hat again and bowed in her direction. She didn't respond, not even to incline her head, but she held his gaze for a moment longer before turning away.

Anything, Cam wanted to shout to her. It didn't much matter what. All she had to do was ask and Cam knew he'd fall all over himself trying to give her her heart's desire. But he didn't. Enough people were watching as it was. Hopefully no one recognized him from the wanted posters.

With her chin pointed toward the sky, she swept inside the bank. For some reason, it looked like she was riding off to battle.

Hell.

Whatever was in the bank wasn't good for the young lady. Cam's instincts told him to turn back, to follow her in. She needed protection or, barring that, backup. She shouldn't have to fight her battles alone.

Hatfield elbowed him in the ribs and gave him a scowl.

"Yeah, I know," Cam grumbled, turning away from the bank again. His protective instincts had gotten them in hot water on more than one occasion. Hatfield still hadn't forgiven him for the time they'd held up a stagecoach far outside of San Antonio with a lovely young woman and her equally lovely mother inside. They'd relieved the ladies of their jewels and taken the horses only to get two miles away and see an approaching Comanche war party. Cam had insisted they turn around and rescue the ladies. And to be sure, the ladies had been appreciative of that rescue—right until they made San Antonio, where it turned out that the women were the wife and daughter of a corporal with the U.S. Army. They certainly were grateful they'd been rescued from the Comanche, but not so grateful for having been robbed in the first place.

He and Hatfield only made it out of that scrape due to the fact that Hatfield was more slippery than an eel when he needed to be.

Cam shook his head. The problem with being a notorious stagecoach robber was the notoriety. It didn't matter how lovely that girl was or how much she looked like she needed a knight in shining armor. She was soft and pampered and clearly above him. Maybe if Cam had a piece of land where he could raise horses—strong horses equipped to deal with the trials of the cattle trails—then maybe...

Hell, who was he kidding? Even a horse breeder wouldn't be good enough for a lady like that.

But he couldn't get past the way she'd braced herself before going into the bank. Whatever or whomever she fought against was in that bank. An idea began to form in his mind.

The man who wanted to hire him and Hatfield had a plan. A large deposit of cash was being sent to the bank by the railroad. It would get here in two weeks in a heavily guarded shipment. The railroad branched out from Brimstone, sending one fork south and one fork due west. That cash was supposed to pay for labor and materials for the next six months.

Their would-be employer wanted the bank robbed on a certain date. He had train schedules, safe combinations, getaway plans—the whole thing planned down to the minute. But the plan called for the robbery to take place three weeks after the money was deposited. There was a lag time there that Cam didn't quite understand. Why wait? Why not hit the train with the money on it, or the wagons delivering it from the train station to the bank? Why wait until it was all locked up in a safe?

It didn't make sense. The plan was good, but it took the path of most resistance.

"What if we robbed it early?" He kept his voice low as a man in a beaver top hat cut a wide path around them.

Hatfield cocked his head, listening.

"It's a good plan," Cam admitted. "Solid. But I don't like doing it on his timeline. What if we agree to take the job and do it ahead of schedule?"

Hatfield worried his lower lip. The two of them had been riding together for almost two years now. Cam had happened across the boy barely holding off three grown men in a darkened alley in Dodge City. Hat couldn't have been more than fourteen then, quick with a blade. But he'd brought a knife to a gunfight and he was about to lose. Cam had ended that fight without hesitation and Hatfield had been by his side ever since. It worked out well that the boy was handy with a gun and had sharp eyes and better ears.

One day, the kid would grow whiskers. Cam would be sorry when the day came, because then Hatfield would be a man in his own right and he wouldn't need Cam to watch out for him.

Cam glanced back at the bank. No, not back at the bank—back to where he'd last seen the pretty miss. It took everything he had not to follow her inside and make sure she was okay.

He needed a woman and a bottle of whiskey, in that order.

He slapped Hatfield on the back and said, "Come on. You ever heard of the Jeweled Ladies? Supposed to be the most famous brothel in Texas and they have hot baths. I'll buy you a woman tonight."

Hatfield gave him a long look and then, without breaking eye contact, spat another stream of tobacco into the street.

Cam rolled his eyes. Hatfield was practically an angel when it came to women. He was good in a knife fight but terrible in a brothel. "Fine. I'll buy you a drink and *I'll* get a woman." It wouldn't be the same as holding that young lady, but it'd be close enough. Probably. "Deal?"

Hatfield gave a swift nod and together, they headed off down the street.

But Cam looked over his shoulder, just one last time.

She wasn't there.

Chapter Two

My dear," Vincent Brown said in that condescending tone that made Cynthia's skin crawl. He hadn't bothered to stand when Cynthia had walked into his office and he still sat, as if she were merely a customer late with the mortgage payment instead of his future wife. "I'm afraid I don't understand."

She kept her face pleasantly blank. "Mr. Brown—Vincent," she said, trying to sound placating instead of furious. "Can we not be frank? While I hold you in the highest respect, I do not have any tender feelings for you and correct me if I'm wrong, but I do not believe that you harbor any tender feelings for me, either."

His lips twisted, as if he found the concept of feelings, tender or otherwise, humorous. "I don't see what that has to do with anything. You have quite an expansive dowry and your father promises me that you come to the marriage pure and unsullied. Tender feelings, as you say, can come later."

If they came at all. She tried to match his amused look, but she saw the way his eyes darkened. Did he like it when she begged? Damn. She hadn't seen that coming, but she should have. "Of course I have saved myself for marriage. It's just that—"

16

Vincent shook his head, dismissing her protest before staring at her bosom. "I know you're concerned. But I truly will not mind if you bring your deranged sister with you. Your father assured me that nothing would bring you as much joy as having your sister be such an important part of our marriage."

Bile rose up in the back of Cynthia's throat. Just because she was a virgin didn't mean she didn't understand what Vincent was saying. He meant to have them both. What her sister wanted—what Cynthia wanted—didn't matter. She was nothing more than a possession being handed off from one heartless man to another.

Was there anything that Vincent wanted about her? Was it just her dowry, unfettered access to her sister, and her own maidenhead? Was her virginity truly the only thing about her as a person that was worth anything to this man? To any man?

"I'm glad we had this talk," Vincent said, leering at her bosom again. "Shall I come around tonight for dinner? Perhaps you lovely sister could join us, if she can behave herself. I've only met her once. I feel we should... get to know each other more before the wedding."

White-hot rage burned through her. When had this man seen Sarah? Oh, no—what had he done to her?

The thought of her father letting Vincent into the nursery while Cynthia ran her afternoon errands was absolutely the final straw. Vincent Brown couldn't have her sister. He couldn't have *her*. That's all it came down to. If her innocence were the only thing he valued, well, she wouldn't give it to him. She refused to accept that a horrid marriage to a horrid man was the only life awaiting her.

She'd do anything to get her and her sister away from this man.

She smiled, hoping it was pretty and not filled with anger. "Of course. Thank you so much for taking time out of your busy day to reassure me." Somehow, she got the lie out.

He smiled and waved her away, as if she were little more than a recalcitrant child in need of a nap. "We'll be seeing each other again soon enough."

Not if she could help it.

Cynthia walked swiftly out of the bank, blinking hard against the tears. There was no way out. But she would not cry. Not because of Vincent Brown.

She needed help because she could not let this pass. But who? Who would dare go against her father and Vincent, against the money that made Brimstone work?

Without conscious thought, she looked down the street, but the hard man with the black hair was gone. Even as the thought occurred to her, she brushed it away. She couldn't approach a strange man on the street and ask him to... what? Kidnap her? Kill her fiancé? Somehow spirit both her and her sister away from this Godforsaken town?

Deflower her so that Vincent Brown wouldn't want her anymore?

The idea was laughable. It didn't matter if that man had been courteous and respectful—or that he'd looked at her with something like longing in his eyes. He was a stranger. His offer of assistance had been a polite yet meaningless bit of small talk.

Yes, he'd been handsome, in a rugged and dangerous kind of way. Yes, he'd had his hands on her body—touches that had sent a shiver racing over her skin. But for all she knew, he was a cattle rustler. Or worse.

Besides, there was a risk to that. Even if she spoiled herself, Vincent might still want her. Her *and* Sarah. No, she needed a plan. She needed to rid herself of her innocence and somehow get enough money— money her father did not control—so she could take Sarah away.

Deranged. Cynthia's blood simmered. Sarah was not deranged. Her mind had just never grown up with her body. She was a child still, after all these years. Cynthia had long ago accepted that she always would be. Which meant Sarah would always need a mother or, barring that, a sister.

Cynthia had twenty-seven days.

A flash of scarlet drew her eye. Lady Ruby, the scandalous owner of the Jeweled Ladies, was making her way down the street with several of her Jewels trailing behind. The woman was sin personified. The cut of her gown was scandalously low and slit up to her knee, to say nothing of the scarlet red color. Rubies dripped from her ears and neck, of course they did. And her hat! Cynthia felt the shallow longing for that fabulous confection of pink and purple silk and dyed feathers.

The realization hit her so hard and fast that she actually stumbled backwards. She needed to rid herself of her virginity? She needed enough money to secure her and Sarah's safety—money her father did not control?

Lady Ruby just might be her salvation.

The women stopped at the baker's, which would hopefully give Cynthia time to catch up to them. She did not want to look like she was racing after the town's most notorious whore. She kept her steps slow and careful, although her mind sped ahead.

Those Jewels, they were of a different sort of woman. They weren't slatternly prostitutes with no sense of morals or style. But they weren't respectable wives and mothers either. They were, Cynthia supposed, businesswomen. Successful businesswomen who did not rely on the protection of a man. No one decided for them what they could and could not do. If they wanted to lift their skirts in the middle of the street, they would—she'd seen it once, when she'd been about fifteen. She didn't remember why the Jewel in a deep shade of amber had flashed her garters. Cynthia only remembered staring in shock at the woman's legs, at her defiant attitude.

Defiance—that was what she needed. A great deal of it.

She stepped into the baker's. The low murmur of feminine voices trailed off as Cynthia's eyes adjusted to the interior.

Perhaps she was vain, just a little. Because the other thing about the Jewels that she admired—had *always* admired—was the way they dressed. Scandalously, to be sure. But their dresses were of the highest quality, the most daring fashion. They'd been the first to do away with bustles in town. Cynthia had been copying their styles for years.

They were free to do whatever they wanted. This was not the first time Cynthia had been jealous of that freedom.

"Oh!" she said in mock surprise, as if she had just realized that the bakery was busy. How was one to approach a madam for this sort of conversation? She had to be careful because if there was anything suspicious, word would get back to her father in the blink of an eye and that would make things difficult.

But Lady Ruby merely turned. Her girls parted so that the madam could speak directly to Cynthia. "Miss Hobbs, that is a fetching outfit you're wearing today."

Cynthia exhaled. She could talk dresses. Clothing was one of the few indulgences her father allowed her, mostly because it reflected on his generous nature and wealth. "Thank you. And may I just say that your hat is one of the loveliest I've ever seen?"

Something shifted in Lady Ruby's eyes. Cynthia couldn't quite read the emotion, but she hoped it was amusement. After all, it wasn't every day that the banker's daughter talked with the most famous whore in Texas. "Thank you, dear."

Taking a deep breath, Cynthia looked around. Aside from the four other Jewels—one who looked Native and wore a stunning shade of turquoise, a white woman with jet black hair in a different shade of red, plus a black woman in light pink and the last, a pale blonde in jade green—the place was empty. Well, except for the baker himself. Cynthia gave Lady Ruby another broad smile that she hoped communicated the need to talk in private.

"Mr. Johnson," Lady Ruby said, turning away from Cynthia. "Do you have any of those little fairy cakes? You know the ones I mean. I see there aren't any out here, but I do so want some. Could you check in the back, please?"

Cynthia almost snorted in the most unladylike way because she knew that voice. She had used it countless times. It was a very effective voice that almost always got her what she wanted—in public, anyway.

The baker's cheeks darkened. "I don't think I have any fresh today... "

"Could you check?" It wasn't a question. Cynthia had to cough and hide her smile behind her hand.

The baker nodded and disappeared in the back. As if by some unspoken command, the Jewels all moved. The Jewel in turquoise stepped behind Cynthia and stood by the front door. The one in pink moved toward the door through which Mr. Johnson had disappeared. The other two moved themselves to respectable distances.

It all happened in seconds. Suddenly Cynthia had something close to privacy with Lady Ruby. She might only have a minute. "I need help."

Lady Ruby lifted an eyebrow. "What do you think I could do for you? You're a respectable young lady and I am... well," she simpered. "We all know what I am."

"My father wants me to marry Vincent Brown in less than a month. Mr. Brown will also become the guardian of my sister."

Lady Ruby's brow tightened and Cynthia was aware she suddenly had the older woman's undivided attention. "I wasn't aware you had a sister."

"I do. She's eighteen, although she has the mind of a four-year-old. Mr. Brown's intentions are not honorable. Not to either of us," she added, unable to keep the bitterness out of her voice.

Lady Ruby's brows moved up. "This all sounds very tragic, but what does it have to do with me?"

Cynthia glanced back to where the Jewel in pink was standing in the doorway. She was asking the baker about something else. Time was running short. "I want to sell my virginity. I'll... I'll split the profits with you. I need enough to take Sarah away from here. Away from *them*."

Point of fact, she had no idea what the monetary value of her virginity was. But surely she could get at least a hundred dollars? Even fifty dollars would be enough to get them away from here. But hopefully not less. The rest... she could sell her mother's jewelry, if she had to.

She looked at Lady Ruby's hat again. Certainly not less than fifty dollars. Hats like that did not come cheap.

"You're serious," Lady Ruby mused, her voice low and sensual.

"My father and Mr. Brown labor under the impression that the only thing of value about me is my innocence. And I don't want to waste that on Vincent Brown."

This caused Lady Ruby's lips—perfectly painted in a deep red color—to form an *O*. Cynthia took some small measure of pride that she'd managed to shock the madam. Surely that wasn't easy to do.

"This is a drastic step, Miss Hobbs. What you're proposing is something that cannot be undone."

"Neither can marriage," she hissed.

Lady Ruby looked amused by this. "When is the wedding scheduled?"

Cynthia almost exhaled in relief. But she didn't.

Not yet. "Twenty-seven days. I only found out yesterday."

Behind her, the Jewel in pink was making another demand of the baker—but Cynthia could hear him getting flustered. Time was almost up. What if this didn't work? What if Lady Ruby refused?

What would Cynthia do?

Lady Ruby turned back to the display case. The Jewel in turquoise stepped around Cynthia, and the other Jewels closed in around her. The meeting was over. Cynthia began to despair, but then Lady Ruby said quietly, "I'll make some arrangements. You'll be hearing from me."

"Soon?"

Mr. Johnson walked out of the back. Lady Ruby nodded, although her attention was on the baker as she made sad noises about cake.

Soon wasn't soon enough.

Chapter Three

O h, God," Lady Ruby moaned, pressing her face against the mattress. "Harder. Harder!"

Cam smacked her on the ass as he pounded into her sweet pussy. The madam of the Jeweled Ladies had taken one look at him and made him the kind of offer that he'd have to be insane to refuse. And Cam didn't like to think he was insane.

She was a beautiful woman, fiery red hair that perfectly matched the red silk corset he hadn't even bothered to unlace. He grabbed hold of those laces now and pulled her back into his chest. "You need something more, my lady?"

Without waiting for an answer, he thrust his hand down between her legs, searching for that little button, the one that held *so* much potential. Splitting his fingers into a V, he stroked down over her pussy, around where he was buried deep inside of her, getting his fingers slick with her cream. She whimpered when the heel of his hand hit her button.

"Oh, yes," he hissed against her neck. "You need more than a good fuck, don't you? You need to be properly finished and I know just how to do it."

She couldn't even nod. Her body shuddered down onto his hand, his cock, and he knew that she was close.

Careful to keep from pulling out, he sank his other hand into her hair and turned her head to the side, exposing that pretty neck of hers. He let his teeth scrape over her skin without biting too hard. It wouldn't do to mark her because she wasn't his to mark.

God, but she felt good. She reached over her head and sank her fingers into his hair, holding him against her. He couldn't thrust is deeply from this angle, but he could feel her muscles tightening around him, feel her crisis getting ready to break.

She yanked his head forward, crushing his lips against hers as her cream flooded his hand and she groaned deep in the back of her throat. She shuddered against him and then her body went limp.

He had no doubt that the madam of the Jeweled Ladies brothel was adept at faking satisfaction for the benefit of her clients. But Cam knew there was no faking *that*.

His stones tightened as he bent her back over the bed and grabbed her hips in both hands. He pounded into her over and over, spreading her wide so that she could take all of him in. He wished he were strong enough to hold off until she broke again—but he wasn't. Not when she squeezed tight against him. He exploded into the sheath she'd made him put on and then collapsed on top of her, both of them breathing hard.

"God, I needed that," he said, rolling off her and closing his eyes.

But even as he did so, the woman he saw in his mind's eye was not the woman he had just fucked senseless. It was the young lady from the street, the one who had gone off to do battle with the bank.

It probably wasn't right—or even all that generous to his current partner—to be thinking about another woman, but Cam was powerless to stop. What would that proper miss do if she were to ever find herself in bed with a man like him? She was an innocent, of that he had no doubt. Would she insist on dousing the lights? Hiding under the sheets? Would she lie there, wishing she were anywhere else, with anyone else?

Or would Cam be able to bring a blush to her cheeks? If he were slow and careful—and for a woman like that, he would be—would he be able to stoke the fires of desire? Would he be able to strip her down and explore her body, maybe for the first time? Would he make her squirm beneath him, her hips rising to meet his thrusts, her body asking for the release that he could give her? Would he leave her panting and sated with a smile on her face?

It was a damn shame he'd never get answers to those questions.

"Where have you been?" Lady Ruby said, swinging a bare arm over his chest. He picked up her hand and kissed it—not so much a gesture of tenderness, but an apology for thinking about the blonde woman.

Cam shrugged. "Around."

"Well," Lady Ruby said, sitting up and smacking him playfully on the chest. "Anytime you're around here, you come back and see me. I haven't been fucked so well in months."

With his cleaner hand, he cupped her face. "Doesn't anyone ever take care of you? A lady as fine as you are should have a veritable stud farm at her command."

"Oh, I knew I liked you," she said, leaning forward to press a kiss to his cheek. Then her nimble fingers removed the sheath from his now-limp cock. "You need a bath, however—and a shave."

He pushed himself up on his elbows, watching her walk into the bathroom and bend over the tub to start the water flowing. "Dare I trust you with a straight razor on my neck?"

She shot him a saucy grin over her shoulder. It was a hell of a view. "I have a very steady hand and I haven't come that hard in far too long. You think I'd endanger a repeat performance?"

He grinned wildly. He liked to see his lovers well satisfied and happy. Also, he wouldn't mind that bath and shave. It was a crying shame he couldn't get Hatfield into the tub. The boy stank to high heaven. But he couldn't. The kid was down in the saloon of the Jeweled Ladies, nursing his whiskey and probably cheating at poker. Hatfield only lost when he thought it wise. As best Cam could tell, that was why he'd been cornered in the alley all those years ago. He hadn't let those other men win enough to make it seem like he wasn't cheating.

Lady Ruby scrubbed Cam from head to toe, making sure his cock was extra clean. She did so nude, which gave Cam the pleasure of watching her tits sway with her every move. "Been here long? You're younger than I thought." He'd heard that the Mistress of the Jeweled Ladies was—well, maybe not old. But definitely older.

She wrapped a warm towel around his face. "I took over for the former Mistress a few months back. But I've been here for almost a year. Lean back."

He whistled as she patted his face with a towel and began to spread the lather on. "Ambitious. I knew I liked you. If there's ever anything I can do for you, my lady, please don't hesitate to let me know." Because a woman with this kind of power was always a good friend to have.

She stood over him, gloriously naked and a bemused smile on her face. "And here I took you for a rogue. Never tell me you're secretly a gentleman in disguise?"

"Fine. I won't tell you," he grinned. He hadn't often been called the gentleman. It should have made him feel stuffy and prissy, like a dandy with soft hands.

But again his thoughts went back to the young lady in the street. She was the kind of woman who needed the gentleman—not just in bed, but out of it too. She shouldn't have to go to war by herself.

"My lady," he started, and then stopped because he wasn't sure how to ask the madam of the brothel if she knew one of the proper young misses in town. And even if she did, he couldn't imagine that an innocent miss would welcome help from someone like Lady Ruby.

Lady Ruby scraped the razor expertly over his face and flicked the foam away. "Thinking of your sweetheart?" she asked in a slightly more reserved voice.

He would've smiled, but then she might've cut him. "I did meet someone who caught my eye. But one look at her and I knew we were worlds apart." He couldn't help the melancholy sigh that escaped from his lips.

That was all there was to it. Beautiful young ladies like her had no business being with a stagecoach robber who was thinking of upping the stakes and becoming a bank robber. What could he offer? Not much, really. A life on the run? Sharing a bedroll beside a campfire with Hatfield snoring on the other side?

If they robbed the bank, he might have enough money to make an honest go of it. He always had liked horses. But it wouldn't work. If a young lady like that weren't already married, she would be soon enough. It would take time, maybe even years, before Cam could be in a position where he could make a respectable offer to a respectable miss.

Lady Ruby wiped his face clean and stared down at him. He was tempted to reach out and palm her heavy breasts, maybe pull her back into the tub and have another taste of her. But something in her eyes stayed his hand. "What?"

"You do yourself a disservice, Cam. You have honor and honesty—not to mention a way in the bedroom." She grinned and he grinned back, but then her smile faded. "This is, after all, America. One never knows when one will be able to suddenly change their circumstances."

He thought about what Lady Ruby had said—she hadn't been here very long, but she'd already taken over the brothel. "That something you know a lot about?"

Her satisfied smile was answer enough. "You *will* come back and see me again, won't you? I have a feeling that you and I are going to be good friends."

At that, Cam did pull her down in the water,

kissing and stroking her breasts and her pussy until he was hard for her again. The only reason they got out of the tub was because he needed another sheath. This time, he lay on his back and let Lady Ruby ride him so that he could give her tits the proper attention they deserved.

But through it all, he couldn't stop thinking about that beautiful young lady in the street, of how she'd feel on top of him. Lady Ruby was amazing, but she wasn't that girl.

Lady Ruby was both right and wrong, because Cam did know. He might be good in bed and he might be friends with the madam of the whorehouse, but he would *never* be enough for a girl like that.

Chapter Four

Every night, exhausted from her day of caring for Sarah, and sick with worry, Cynthia fell into bed. Sunday night was no different.

If only she knew how much money she was going to get for this auction, she could plan a little better. She needed to get out of Texas, but where? Somewhere out east? North? She and Sarah could disappear in a city like Chicago. But Chicago felt huge to her. She had no idea how to survive in a city that large. But even that wasn't the first concern she had.

Who would buy her virginity? Who would look at an innocent and decide to debauch her? Would she get an ugly man or a mean one? She wasn't going to submit to Vincent Brown. But...

What if he bought her, anyway?

One night. She could get through one night of anything if it meant she and Sarah could be free for the rest of their lives.

She must've slept because her thoughts drifted away from Vincent and marriage and instead settled on a different man. A man with dark hair and a wicked smile, who held her gently and then tightly. When he put his hands on her breasts—she wasn't wearing anything—she didn't feel afraid. His hands teased her nipples to hard points. Then his hand was between her legs, at that secret spot that throbbed for his caresses. She grabbed his shoulders and laced her fingers through his dark hair as he bent to suckle at her breast.

This was right, she thought dreamily as her body began to hum at a high pitch under his touches. This was how it was supposed to be. But it wasn't enough. She ached for this man, ached for what he was doing to her body. His muscles were hard under her hands as she scrabbled for purchase. But his caresses were soft and maddening and she wanted more. She wanted everything and—

A hand closed over her mouth, pulling her out of the sweet dream. Cynthia startled and tried to scream, but the hand clamped down tighter. Cynthia's eyes came into focus.

There was a woman next to her bed, with shining black hair and brown skin. The woman was wearing a black jacket over what looked like... buckskin? But for all that, she looked familiar. Had Cynthia seen her before? Wasn't she the Jewel in turquoise from the bakery?

The young woman tapped her lips with her fingers, the universal signal for be quiet. When Cynthia nodded, she removed her hand and handed Cynthia a note.

Miss Sky will escort you to the Jeweled Ladies.—R

Cynthia looked at the Native girl. "Are you Miss Sky?"

The girl nodded and crooked her finger, signaling that she wanted Cynthia to follow her. Cynthia nodded and the girl touched her lips again, reminding her to be quiet. Then she held out a pair of men's pants, plus another jacket and a slouch hat.

Cynthia understood. Brimstone was a quiet town on Sunday night, but she had no desire to be caught out of the house. The disguise would be best for everyone.

Quickly, she dressed in the strange clothes. The girl held a pair of boots, but didn't let Cynthia put them on. Instead, she carried them as they silently crept downstairs together. Cynthia expected them to sneak out the back, but instead the girl led her to the dining room, which was directly under her room. The window was open and a late spring breeze ruffled the curtains.

Cynthia shoved her feet into the too-big boots and hurried to the window. She already had one leg over the sill when she realized there was a giant of a man outside. Before she could react, he grabbed her around the waist and set her on the ground as if she weighed nothing at all. Then he did the same for Miss Sky.

Silently, she followed Miss Sky and the giant man as they skulked through the shadows. It was only a matter of minutes until they approached the Jeweled Ladies. Technically, the brothel wasn't open on Sundays and the house was almost dark, save a few dim lights shining out of windows on the upper floors. Together the odd trio slipped around the back and cut through the kitchen.

Cynthia wasn't sure what she expected. Maybe she thought she would be led to an office or a bedroom. Instead the giant peeled off as Miss Sky led her to the dining room. There, clustered around a long table, were thirteen other women. Lady Ruby sat at the head of the table, next to an open seat.

"Ah, there you are. I trust everything went well?" She did not ask Cynthia, but instead directed her question to Miss Sky.

The Native girl nodded and took a seat at the far end of the table.

Cynthia looked nervously around the room. A large clock at the far end showed her that it was only eleven forty-five at night. Late by her standards, but perhaps not by the brothel's.

The girls all looked like... well, like girls. They weren't wearing their rainbow colors that signified their Jewel name. Instead, some were wearing simple day dresses, others had on wrappers. They looked not like expensive whores, but like a group of friends at an afternoon tea.

Cynthia swallowed nervously. Some of the girls looked at her with frank curiosity, some with open hostility. She had a fleeting wish that she had been more polite to the Jewels before now. But then Lady Ruby spoke.

"I believe we all know who our guest is, but while she is within these walls, she will need a different name. I was thinking that we would call her Diamond, as she will be the rarest of the Jewels. But she needs a last name. Any suggestions?"

The girls all spoke at once.

"Shine?"

"Brilliance?"

"White?" The girls debated this. Apparently, there had been a lot of Miss Whites over the years.

When there was a lull in the conversation, a strong voice from the middle of the table said, "Bright," in a voice that brooked no argument.

"Ah," Lady Ruby said, smiling tightly at the woman with the white-blond hair. "Thank you, Pearl. Miss Diamond Bright it is. Now. I know that many of you are wondering why Miss Bright has come to us." Several heads nodded and a few girls looked anxious. Cynthia wished they were wearing the colors because in all honesty, aside from Miss Sky, she didn't recognize anyone right now. Only Lady Ruby was dressed in her signature deep blood red. "I'm going to auction off her virginity to the highest bidder."

Unexpectedly, the girl two-thirds down the table burst into tears. Another girl put her arm around the sobbing woman and made soothing noises.

"Oh, Amethyst—it's not like that," Lady Ruby said, sounding almost sympathetic.

That was when Cynthia realized that the girl had probably been auctioned off against her will.

Pearl, who had suggested her name, cast a hard look at Cynthia. "Then perhaps we should know what it *is* like before we agree to be party to this."

Lady Ruby opened her mouth but Cynthia spoke first. She was so tired of having other people speak for her. "My father arranged for me to be married to Vincent Brown in less than three weeks."

There was a collective gasp from the room and a girl spoke up. "Vincent? But he's… "

"Awful," another girl said. Several girls shuddered in obvious disgust.

Cynthia's stomach twisted hard and she felt like she might be ill. These women might not have a place in society. They might all be damned to Hell for their sins, but they knew what went on between men and women and they knew that marriage to Vincent Brown would be horrific. It wasn't just her. She wasn't imagining things.

Her knees weakened and somehow, she wound up sitting in the chair next to Lady Ruby, who said sympathetically, "Yes, you can see why Miss Bright has sought us out."

Cynthia cleared her throat. "I know it doesn't make any sense. But he's so proud that I'm going to come to this marriage innocent and pure and I thought, why should I waste my purity on him?"

"Quite right," someone said. Cynthia didn't see who had spoken.

"There is one other thing to consider," Lady Ruby went on. She turned to Cynthia and nodded. "Go on, dear."

"I have a sister." The room got very still very quickly. No one shifted in their chairs, no one sighed or gasped. It was almost as if she cast a spell over the room. "She's eighteen and beautiful but she has the mind of a three- or four-year-old. She will always be a child in a woman's body, always need me to take care of her. And so... " Her throat closed up and the words got stuck and she couldn't get them out. She stared down at the polished surface of the table, blinking hard.

"And so her father has agreed to send Miss Bright's sister to Vincent Brown as well," Lady Ruby finished for her.

The silence in the room was oppressive. These were women who worked on their backs or their knees. Cynthia had no idea how they had come to this place, but there were no mysteries for them, no vague allusions.

Everyone in this room understood her dilemma.

"It's just for one night," Cynthia said, unable to keep her voice from breaking and unable to care. "I want it to happen on my terms. My choice. And I need enough money to take Sarah away from here. I need your help." She looked up, reassured by the open, caring faces looking back at her. "Please."

Lady Ruby took Cynthia's hand in hers and gave it a squeeze. "And so you shall have it. This is your last chance to change your mind, however. Once done, this is a thing that cannot be undone. You will never have your innocence back. You will never have a proper wedding night."

Tears pricked her eyes, but she blinked them away and squared her shoulders. "I have thought and thought and *thought* about this since I approached you at the baker's. I don't know that there is another way."

"Why don't you marry someone else?" one of the black girls asked. Cynthia thought she was the Jewel who'd been in pink at the bakery. "Roy Griffin—he'd be suitable for you. He's young, he's good in bed and he's quite rich. He owns the hotel. He's really quite nice."

Shame burned at her cheeks that they knew about Mr. Griffin's skill in the bedroom. "He asked my father for permission to court me several years ago. My father refused."

Another girl opened her mouth, ready with a suggestion of an eligible bachelor in town, but Cynthia shook her head. "He has refused permission to them all. Mr. Delgado, Mr. Baumgartner, especially Mr. Griffin. None of them were good enough for me, he said. He tried to make it sound like he was protecting me. But we all know that's not true anymore. He was saving me," she finished bitterly. "None of them will go against him—he controls the money in this town. He thinks he controls everything. But not me. Not anymore."

Another awkward silence filled the room. Cynthia couldn't look at anyone. What must they think of her? She'd hardly ever acknowledged the Jewels when they passed on the street or met in the dry-goods store. She'd admired their clothes, but she'd kept her thoughts to herself. She'd thought she was too good for them, always.

And here was the truth of it. She was no better than them. She might not ever be.

Lady Ruby clapped her hands and stood, gently pulling Cynthia to her feet. "So we have our heading. The wedding is in nineteen days. I believe that gives us no more than twelve days to prepare. Ten, just to be certain. No one must breathe a word of her true identity outside of this room, nor the identity of her sister. And of course, Miss Bright will need to have her appearance disguised. Suggestions?"

A dark-haired woman close by nodded. "I have a wig to change her look entirely. If we pin it well, it won't come off... "

Another woman with shimmering eyes spoke. "We should dress her in white, obviously. We are selling her purity." She turned to the girl next to her. "Do we still have the dress from Miss Pearl White? That was several years ago, but I don't believe she took it with her."

The other woman, her brown hair hanging in glossy waves down her back, said, "I know where to look." She cast a critical eye at Cynthia's figure. "We might have to take it up and it's sure to be tight around her tits, but it would work."

Cynthia managed not to wince at the crude language. The truth was, her bosom had always been overly large.

"Excellent," Lady Ruby said, a note of pleasure in her voice. "What else?"

"A mask," the girl named Amethyst said, her eyes red. But she'd stopped crying. Cynthia hoped the girl didn't judge her too harshly. "Something that will stay fixed throughout the night, so there are no accidental discoveries."

Lady Ruby smiled broadly. "Good girl. What else? We'll need to advertise our special event, but I trust word-of-mouth will be easy enough to accomplish."

Low conversation hummed around the room, but Cynthia only caught snatches of it. She swallowed and turned to Lady Ruby. There was still one thing that weighed on her. "We'll split the money and you'll help me and Sarah get away?" She didn't want to leave anything to chance.

Lady Ruby's eyes glittered with what Cynthia hoped was amusement and not a warning. "Leave everything to me. In ten days time, Miss Diamond Bright will make her grand debut at the Jeweled Ladies and, the morning after, you and your sister will be safely on your way."

Chapter Five

Y'all here for the auction?" The big black man asked Cam and Hatfield as the door of the Jeweled Ladies shut behind them.

"What auction?" Cam asked, hitching his saddlebags up over his shoulder. He had his guns and bullets in there. They weren't allowed inside the brothel or anywhere else in town, everyone knew that, but he wanted to keep them close. He and Hat were going to slip out the back after they established their alibi with some lovely ladies and then rob a bank.

All in all, it looked to be a good night.

"Big doings," the doorman said. "We got ourselves a virgin tonight. Highest bidder gets to bed her."

Well, that sounded positively barbaric. "What if we are?"

"Two dollars gets you the right to bid."

Cam looked down at Hatfield. The boy's lip curled as if he wanted to spit. Cam sympathized. "He's not interested," he said, jerking his thumb towards his partner. "You got someone nice and quiet for my friend here? Someone shy, like he is? He needs a bath."

Hatfield glared at him, his shoulders tense.

"Sure enough," the doorman said, turning his attention to Hatfield. "Amethyst should suit you fine. And you?"

Cam didn't particularly want to bed a virgin. But never let it be said that he didn't have a curious heart. "Yeah, okay." He dug out the silver pieces. What did it matter? By this time tomorrow, he'd have thousands of dollars.

Besides, what kind of woman auctioned off her virginity? It was ludicrous, that's what it was. These were modern times. He didn't particularly care if a woman was a virgin or not, as long as she was willing.

The doorman motioned him to the saloon side of the brothel. The last time Cam had been here, he'd been fascinated by the place—and by Lady Ruby.

Damn. A special thing tonight meant Ruby probably wouldn't be available. He would've enjoyed making her his alibi.

It didn't matter. Any girl—and any bath—would do.

"You come with me," the big man said, leading Hatfield away. "You stay in the parlor tonight. Amethyst is ready for you."

Cam winked at Hatfield, mostly just to irritate the boy. He was rewarded with a fierce scowl. Then they were gone.

Cam made his way to the bar and ordered a whiskey. The Jeweled Ladies was always busy, but tonight was crazy. There wasn't room for any of the other ladies in the saloon. The men were packed in so tightly there was barely room for him to stand along the bar at the back. Even the tables had been removed to make more room. No one was gambling tonight.

Dandies in beaver top hats stood toe-to-toe with farmers in muddy boots and cowboys of every shape, size and color, and one man wore a fair amount of animal skins. There was a lot of money in this room, Cam could feel it. If he didn't have big plans for the rest of this evening, he might take it upon himself to relieve a few of these idiots of their hard-earned cash when they stumbled home in the early hours of the morning.

But that wasn't the sort of alibi he was looking for. So he nodded to the gentleman behind the bar, wearing a gray suit and a silver waistcoat. "What's all this about, anyway?"

"It's not every day we get a virgin in here," the man admitted. "It's something of a novelty. You looking to buy?"

Cam shook his head. "I like my women with a little more experience."

The bartender snorted and moved on to take another order.

From where he stood, Cam could just see through the hall and into the parlor. There were a lot of beautiful ladies over there and very few gentlemen. Hatfield sat in a prissy pink chair next to a woman swathed in light purple. The girl was petite and delicate, with light brown hair and clear eyes—and she didn't look over seventeen. She batted her eyes at Hatfield and in turn, the boy's face turned bright red. Cam smiled. A man had to have his first at some point and that pretty young lady might be just right for a nervous fellow.

Then Lady Ruby appeared on the small stage at the other end of the saloon, sin dripping off her lips and her hips. Cam smiled at the pleasant memory of burying his cock inside her. But even then, there was a sadness attached to it. He'd had a good time with her. They'd both been satisfied—he'd made sure of that. But aside from that... Nothing.

Instead, his mind turned back to the girl he'd run into the last time they were in town, the one who had gone off to do battle with the bank. Cam couldn't quite imagine laying that young miss out and pounding into her until they were both sweating. It didn't seem quite right, to put her face into his fantasies.

But he'd *felt* something for her, something more than needing a good fuck. That young lady had pulled at him. He wouldn't mind having a little more of that pull.

The Jeweled Ladies was the best—expensive, but clean. The food was good and the baths were better. This was the sort of place a man could lose himself in.

But it would always be something he paid for. Not something he'd earned. Maybe he was getting old, but he wanted to earn that kind of woman.

Idiot. That kind of woman would never be for a man like him so he best put her from his mind now.

"... For joining us on this historic occasion," Lady Ruby was saying.

Cam frowned. She'd been different when she'd been with him, easier and a little softer, more teasing. Right now she seemed almost mercenary. He could appreciate it from a business point of view, but not from an attraction point of view.

"I am pleased to introduce a once-in-a-lifetime opportunity for our most discerning guests. A young lady of great beauty has decided to avail herself of a well-intentioned gentleman for one night and one night only. Only sixteen, she is a complete innocent and therefore, I would suggest that those of you with more exotic fantasies please remove yourself from the saloon and seek out our more experienced Jewels in the parlor. Gentlemen, this girl is no Black Pearl or Peridot Green."

There was a hearty round of laughter and Cam tried to think—who was Black Pearl? Someone scandalous, that much was clear.

Lady Ruby smiled until the laughter died down. "Again, I remind you, this is for one night only. The Jeweled Ladies may never see another event of this magnitude."

Cam rolled his eyes. She was laying it on a little thick, wasn't she?

"Without further ado, allow me to introduce... Miss Diamond Bright!" With that, she stepped aside.

The curtain at the back of the stage parted and out stepped an ethereal creature, with shining black hair that fell in loose waves down to her waist. A mask of sparkling white satin covered the top half of her face. At this distance, Cam couldn't quite make out her eyes, but he thought they might be blue.

Her dress was white and should've been virginal and innocent looking. Yet it was anything but. The neckline cut so far down that Cam was convinced that, by leaning forward, he'd be able to catch the edge of her rosy nipples. And the dress was slit up the side above her knee, just to where he could see a glimpse of a black garter against the white stocking high on her thigh.

Lust slammed into his gut with a force that almost knocked him backwards. If there'd been any room to be knocked backwards. With a strange half smile affixed to her face, the girl stepped out to the edge of the stage, lifted her chin, and looked around the room. Men were moaning and groaning, whistling and hooting as if she were a prize to be won at a county fair. But the girl didn't act as if she heard the noise at all. She merely squared her shoulders, like she was getting ready to do battle. Like—

Their gazes collided across the crowded room and a jolt of recognition hit Cam square in the chest. *Like the girl.* The blond, innocent girl in deep purple who'd been going to do battle at the bank. But this creature—she wasn't blond and she didn't look all that innocent. Not with her generous tits practically spilling out of her dress. Not to mention the garters.

Was it possible this was the same girl? He whipped his hat off his head and covered his heart with it, nodding in her direction. He couldn't be sure, but he thought her eyes widened a little. Then she lowered her chin in an ever-so-slight nod before her gaze moved on.

There was a large man on the floor just in front of the stage. He was pushing the crowd back, making sure the girl had a safe space. Cam was glad of it because this was the kind of crowd that could turn into a violent mob in a heartbeat and he would not be party to a gang rape. Thank God Ruby wouldn't either.

Lady Ruby stepped to the front, her gaze severe. Cam half expected her to pull a pistol and fire it into the air. "Gentlemen—honestly. I expected better of you. Beau? Do up your trousers and have a seat immediately or I *will* have Mr. Steel remove you."

At Lady Ruby's harsh tone, the crowd quieted.

"That's better. We are not animals here at the Jeweled Ladies and anyone who would treat Miss Bright thusly will find themselves permanently barred from our establishment. Am I making myself clear?"

That got everyone else to shut the hell up. Being barred from the Jeweled Ladies was a travesty.

Cam glanced into the parlor. He didn't see Hatfield or the girl in purple. Good. Hopefully, that boy was getting a bath, if nothing else.

"Now," she went on, "shall we opened the bidding? One night, which, it should be noted, ends at three a.m. One night to introduce Miss Bright to the pleasures of carnal pursuits."

"I'll give you fifty dollars for her," a man in a greasy slouch hat said, surging to his feet. He looked like a farmer, and not a clean one.

A ripple of excitement moved over the crowd. A white cowboy in front of Cam leaned over to whisper something in the ear of the black man next to him. The black man shook his head and then the two of them made their way out of the parlor.

Another man scoffed. "A hundred and fifty dollars." Cam couldn't see who'd spoken, but from the cultured tone of his voice, he was a rich bastard. "Sit down, Jethro. You're out of your league here."

There was a round of laughter as Jethro whipped off his hat and shook his fist at the dandy.

Cam studied the girl on stage. She might as well have been a statue—she was that still and that proud. *So brave*, he thought.

"Two hundred dollars," another man said. This was closely followed by, "two hundred and twenty-five."

A ripple of unease went through the crowd. This was serious money, more than most of these men probably saw in a year. And they'd only been at this for five minutes.

"Too rich for my blood," Jethro grumbled. "I'm going over to the other side. I'd rather have a woman who knows what to do with her mouth, anyway." Several other men followed him out. Cam could hear the excited coos of the Jewels in the parlor, welcoming the promise of that fifty dollars.

The crowd had thinned out just enough that Cam was able to move forward. He got halfway to the stage. Closer to her. It had to be her, the same girl he'd held in the shelter of his arms to keep from getting hurt. The same girl he'd felt that urge to protect from the bank.

"Three hundred dollars."

"Three fifty."

Cam studied the girl. Closer now, he could see how her chest was rising and falling rapidly, as if she couldn't get enough air. Why was she doing this? Why was she selling herself to the highest bidder? Why would anyone *choose* this?

"Four hundred." A few more people groaned, but no one made the move to leave. The remaining crowd wanted to see how this ended.

Cam had five hundred dollars in his saddlebag, wrapped in a cloth and tucked next to his pistol. That was half of what they were to be paid for robbing the bank, the other half upon completion. It didn't feel right to wager that on one night with the girl. He was supposed to split this money with Hatfield. But did it matter? If things went right, they would high-tail it out of town with ten times that amount to their name. Cam could buy a piece of land and some horses and maybe live an honest life for once.

"Four hundred and fifteen." This from the man that Cam thought Lady Ruby had told to sit down and do up his pants, as if he were going to hop up on stage and deflower the girl in front of seventy-five salivating bastards.

The girl—Diamond—flushed a deep red from her cheeks all the way down to her tits. Was it anger? Or fear? For her sake, Cam hoped it was anger. He didn't want her to be afraid.

"Four hundred and twenty." This from a man with a waxed mustache and pristine white ten-gallon hat.

"Four hundred and twenty-five," the first man said, but he said it through gritted teeth, as if an additional five dollars at this point were going to break him.

Hatfield would kill Cam. The boy would shoot him and then stab him—and then maybe shoot him again, just to be sure.

The man in the white hat paused before aiming a malicious smile at his competitor. "Four hundred and thirty. Give it up, Beau. We both know you don't have that kind of cash in the bank. And your buddy Hobbs got called out of town on an emergency, didn't he? So he can't give you an emergency loan. You can't get anything, can you?"

Beau surged to his feet, but the big man protecting Miss Bright grabbed him by his shoulder and sat him down hard. The man in the white hat looked smug. "That's it, isn't it? No one else can afford Miss Bright." He stood and looked around the room. "I own her. She's mine."

Cam was not imagining the shiver that raced over Miss Bright's body at the man's words.

No one said anything. No one challenged this man's dominance. Not even Lady Ruby. Her smile was tight, but faked. Cam had seen her up close with a real smile on her face and this wasn't it.

Hatfield was just going to have to kill him because Cam couldn't let this bastard lay a hand on that girl. "Five hundred dollars," he called out into the stunned silence. The high bidder swung around in shock, but Cam didn't hide.

It was a hell of a price to pay if he were wrong and Miss Diamond up there wasn't the same girl as at the bank. But then, if she wasn't—so what? Just because he didn't know her didn't mean he wanted her first time to be with some heartless bastard who thought that paying for a few hours of her time meant he *owned* her, for God's sake.

The girl's gaze snapped to him and she inclined her head gracefully in acknowledgment. Lady Ruby sighed and said, "Five hundred dollars. Mr. Douglas, that's quite generous." She turned to the man in the white hat. "Mayor James, would you care to increase your bid?"

The entire room held its breath. Cam knew he was holding his.

If the mayor—the mayor!—outbid him, Cam wasn't sure what he would do. Both Ruby and Diamond seemed visibly relieved at his offer. If he outbid the mayor a second time, would Lady Ruby consider anything over five hundred dollars a short-term loan until he could pay her back? He didn't exactly want to tell the madam that he was going to rob the bank in the wee hours of the morning, but he could get the money to her quickly. And she knew him, after all. She knew he'd treat the girl well. That had to count for something, right?

The mayor stared him down. "I don't believe you've got the money for this girl," he drawled, his eyes sinister. The space between them cleared out a little bit, as if the men were looking for a brawl to break out.

Dimly, Cam realized he was working on a hell of an alibi. "I don't believe I have to prove anything to you," he said, launching a smile in the direction of the women on the stage. "Just them. They're the ones who matter, aren't they?"

At that, Beau chuckled and slapped his leg. "Serves you right, you sonofabitch," he said to the mayor. Then Beau turned to Cam. "You got balls, son. But I'd recommend watching them."

Cam touched the brim of his hat in acknowledgment of this warning, then made his way to the stage. He brushed right past the mayor, refusing to show fear. The man had the good sense not to touch him, but he hissed, "You made an enemy today, boy."

Cam winked because he knew it would drive the mayor crazy. But his attention was on Lady Ruby and Miss Bright. He whipped his hat off his head and bowed at the waist. "Ladies, may I say you both look radiant tonight."

Behind him, someone snorted in disgust. Cam ignored it.

Then Lady Ruby said, "Mr. Steel?" and the big

51

man in front of the stage pushed through the crowd. He began carrying the tables back in. The bar began to do a hopping business. And then, the remaining Jewels who weren't already taken for the night came flooding into the saloon, beautiful women in colored dresses that would've caught anyone's eye.

Anyone but his. Up close now, Cam could see the girl's eyes—and they were the pretty blue color that he remembered from that day in the street. Her hair was wrong, but everything else was right. He could *feel* it.

She gave him a tremulous smile. That was when he realized she'd lost whatever the battle she'd had in the bank and lost badly. That had somehow led her here.

It'd led her right to him.

Chapter Six

It was *him*. The man she'd seen on the street a few weeks ago, the one who'd knocked her down and then told her he'd make it up to her.

Somehow, she didn't think this was what he'd meant.

He'd bought her. She was terrified, but she probably would have been terrified no matter what. At least she didn't know this man, beyond a memorable moment of eye contact. She wasn't sure how she would've gotten through the night if the mayor himself had been the winner, to say nothing of haughty Beau Haughton, one of her father's oldest friends—and a man she had known since childhood. A man who had forced more than one terrifying kiss on her before she'd been able to get away.

"Shall we?" Lady Ruby said, motioning with a nod of her head for the gentleman—Mr. Douglas—to come up on stage and follow them back through the door hidden behind the curtain.

"By all means, we shall, my lady," he said and then he aimed a saucy wink at her.

She tried to smile back, but it was beyond her. She hoped her hand wasn't trembling too much when he winged his arm out to her. Lady Ruby held the curtain aside and they went through the hidden door, stepping down in the kitchen. Cynthia was almost overwhelmed by the heat and noise and the smells of food. She hadn't been able to eat anything today, she'd been so nervous. Even now, the scent of fried chicken turned her stomach.

The moment the door was closed behind them, cutting them off from the stage and the men who'd bid on her, Lady Ruby exhaled heavily. "Thank goodness that's over."

"Everything go okay?" the big black woman cooking the chicken asked without looking over her shoulder.

"Quite well," Lady Ruby said, turning a warm smile on the man standing next to Cynthia. "Cam, darling, I'm so glad to see you. I didn't know you were planning on coming. Do you actually have five hundred dollars on you?"

"My lady, you injure my pride." He acted as if Lady Ruby had shot him through the heart. He pulled his arm away from Cynthia so he could rummage around in his saddlebag. "Point of fact, I do. It's all here. If that mayor of yours had outbid me, though, I would've had to ask for the rest to be considered a loan."

Cynthia stiffened. She couldn't wait for a loan to be repaid. She was leaving in eight hours, never to return to Brimstone—or Texas, for that matter.

Lady Ruby gave her a comforting smile. "I would have extended you the credit—but don't let that get around. Follow me." She moved to where a butler's staircase led up the back of the house on the other side of the kitchen—the same one Cynthia had been snuck up four hours earlier so she could be transformed into Miss Diamond Bright.

So Lady Ruby knew this man? Was that a good thing?

"I found myself in the neighborhood." He reached over and covered Cynthia's hand with his. Then he leaned close, his breath brushing her ear. It wasn't sour or rancid. She caught a hint of whiskey, but underneath that was... mint? He'd brushed recently, thank goodness. "Breathe," he whispered as they followed Lady Ruby upstairs.

She forced herself to take a deep breath and then another one, her chest straining against her corset, the silk mask rubbing against her nose. This was happening. This was really happening. But five hundred dollars! That would leave her two hundred and fifty dollars, once Lady Ruby took her half. That was more than enough for her and Sarah to get away.

She glanced up at the ceiling, although there was no way she could see the quiet attic room where Sarah was currently hiding. Lady Ruby had insisted on bringing the girl into the brothel. That way, if something went wrong, she'd said, the sisters would be together and she could protect them. But Cynthia was worried. She would feel better if Doreen was sitting with Sarah, but... there was too much risk bringing the maid into this. Hopefully, Sarah was asleep. If she weren't...

Mr. Douglas made a noise, almost a crooning sound and oddly, Cynthia was soothed. She could worry about Sarah later. She had five hours with this man that she had to get through first.

"Cam, I trust you recall the rules?"

"Of course, my lady."

Cynthia glanced up at him—he was quite tall—and was almost amused to see a look of indignation on his face.

"You know I would never do anything to hurt a woman."

"Yes, I am rather relieved about that, as is Miss Bright, I'm sure. Ah, here we are." They came out at the back of the house, right next to Lady Ruby's room. Which was to be Cynthia's room for the night.

"I'm sure you remember your way around," Lady Ruby said, unlocking the door. Cynthia would not be locked in and Mr. Steel, the man who'd guarded the stage downstairs, would be close at hand in case Cynthia screamed.

Then Cynthia realized what Lady Ruby had just said. *Oh.* Mr. Douglas had been with Lady Ruby before. An uneasy feeling tightened around her chest. Of course she hadn't expected Mr. Douglas to be some innocent like she was. She'd known that any man who would buy a virgin at auction was a man who frequented whorehouses. But the thought that this man had lain with Lady Ruby in this very room...

She should be relieved because it was clear Lady Ruby liked Mr. Douglas and trusted him. Cynthia was lucky her first time would be with someone who knew what he was doing, someone who doffed his hat for a lady and saved her from the mayor and Beau Haughton.

And Mr. Douglas was quite handsome, in his rough way. He was big but he moved with an easy grace—a grace that had been haunting her dreams. This was the best of all possible outcomes.

Lady Ruby opened the door to her room and Mr. Douglas escorted Cynthia inside. "Lady Ruby? My friend Hatfield is with Miss Amethyst, I believe. Hopefully he's getting a bath. If he asks where I am... "

Lady Ruby inclined her head, ever the gracious hostess. "Of course, Cam. We'll make sure that your friend is well taken care of. Should you two need anything at all, don't hesitate to ask." She looked to Cynthia, waiting.

Breathe. Cynthia inclined her head and said in a low, husky voice she'd practiced just in case she did wind up with someone she knew, "Thank you, Lady Ruby."

Then the madam was gone, the door shut behind her.

She and Mr. Cam Douglas stood there for a moment, frozen. At least she was frozen. She'd received very little instruction as to what would happen next. There'd been debate amongst the Jewels, but they had universally agreed that if she knew too much, her gentleman caller might not believe she was innocent and then demand his money back.

She shifted, wondering if she could really feel the silver dollar that had been inserted inside of her or if she was just imagining the cold, heavy metal. Lady Ruby had said that her caller would use a sheath, but it never hurt to be prepared. A silver dollar placed far inside of her would help keep her safe. Cynthia had no idea how, but she trusted Lady Ruby in this. Inserting the silver dollar, however, had been one of the most mortifying experiences of her life.

Or at least, it had been until right now. Mr. Douglas came to stand in front of her. Somehow, instead of her hand resting on his arm, he now held it in his giant hand. "What did they do to your hair?"

Cynthia's eyes went wide. "Excuse me?"

"Blond, wasn't it? Blond and in curls?" He tilted his head to the side and ran his fingers over her forehead. "It's not bad. But I like it better blond."

Her heart about stopped. "You know who I am?"

He stepped back and gave her a crooked smile even as he began to untie the bandanna from around his neck. "But that's just it, isn't it? I don't. I ran into you on the street. You were beautiful then. You're beautiful now," he added before Cynthia could say anything. "But you look like a Jewel and you're not, are you?"

She stared at the little bit of neck he'd unveiled as he dropped the bandanna to the floor. "I am for tonight."

"I'm Cam. Cam Douglas. But you probably picked up on that. And you are... "

Lady Ruby had made it explicitly clear that so long as she was within these walls, she had no other name. "Miss Diamond Bright." She tried to smile, but she knew it was shaky. She'd been reassured by Lady Ruby and the Jewels that her nervousness was not a cause for concern. It just demonstrated that she was what she said she was—a virgin.

"Sure." He sat down and kicked off his boots, then peeled off his socks. Should she be doing something? She had no idea. She was just standing there, like a bump on a log, overthinking everything. The girls had promised her that she might enjoy this. They had warned her about the pinch of pain, but several said it was really quite lovely.

"Should I... should I help you? Get undressed?"

"Don't rush yourself, darlin'. We're going to have a bath first. Ah, I see Lady Ruby left some wine.

Bath, then wine. And then we'll see what happens, all right? I don't want to do anything to upset you." He stood, shrugging out of his jacket.

She couldn't help the nervous laugh that burst from her at that. "I volunteered for this. I want—" Her voice hitched. "I want what you want."

He paused. "You need the money, I think. But you don't need this."

The laugh got stuck in her throat, and suddenly, she was on the verge of crying. "No," she said, her voice shaking. "You don't understand. I need to be ruined. And you have paid for the right to do that. So ruin me. Throw me down and do it and get it over with."

His eyebrows had risen during this awkward speech, his hands frozen on his suspenders. "I've changed my mind."

In that moment, Cynthia almost died. If he walked out of this room and took back his money, where would she be? Right back where she started. Maybe the mayor…

"Wine first, *then* bath," Cam said decisively. "I'll take you if you want, darlin', but I can't make love to a woman who's in hysterics." He pulled his suspenders down and then tugged the hem of his shirt out of his pants. Before Cynthia could brace herself, he pulled the whole thing over his head and stood before her bare-chested.

For a second, she forgot how to breathe. He was broad, without an ounce of fat on him. A faint dusting of dark hair covered his chest and then trailed lower in a line that disappeared below the waist of his pants.

She'd never seen a man undressed before. It was shockingly intimate and a strange sort of heat flooded her body, making her shiver. He was powerfully built—and probably nothing like what Vincent Brown looked like without his clothes. Cam was carved from granite, with a few scars that told of a life of danger, one on his shoulder and one by his ribs.

"Can you take the mask off?" he asked in a low voice as his hands went to the buttons on his trousers.

"I'm... " It took her a moment to drag her gaze away from his chest. When she finally looked back at his face, he had a bemused smile for her. "I'm not supposed to."

"Ah," he said as another button gave. "But that was to hide who you are." Another button. "And we've established that I don't know who you are, my darlin' girl. It will be easier, I think, without it."

He was on the last button now, his trousers hanging loosely off his hips. Another burst of warmth fired through her body, and her lips parted. She was his for the night but that meant he was hers, too—didn't it? She could touch that chest, touch all of him and hardly give a second thought to the consequences.

For just one night, she could live another life, one of wild abandon and none of the rules that governed her every movement. She could be selfish and take pleasure in this man. She could embrace sinning, and tomorrow she could go back to being responsible and in charge. Tonight would all be a dream.

This must be why Lady Ruby had been so relieved. Cam Douglas was a man who could make even a virgin burn with lust.

She turned away and began fumbling with the mask. The Jewel named Garnet had firmly pinned it into place underneath the wig so that neither could be pulled off. "Do you think anyone else recognized me?" she asked, hating the way her voice wavered.

Because if so, that was even worse. Word might get back to her father sooner rather than later and it would make leaving with Sarah before dawn that much more difficult.

"No. I didn't hear anyone use a name. I only figured it out because I recognized the way you squared your shoulders. I saw you do the same thing before you walked into the bank."

Suddenly there was warmth against her back and his hands burrowed under the wig, finding the pins and pulling them free. "I recognized the way you carried yourself," he said, his voice low and soft in her ear. She tensed but at the same time she wanted to relax back into him. "I recognized your determination, your bravery. I recognized your willingness to fight. Nothing else," he said, bumping his hips against hers.

Cynthia felt something long and hard against her backside and she blushed, innocent that she was.

"No one else sees how strong you are, do they?"

She shut her eyes to keep the tears from pooling, as hairpins scattered onto the floor around them. She had been told she was beautiful more times than any one person could count. She was vain enough to appreciate the compliment, but this? No one had ever seen beyond her face, her hair, her bosom.

It was possible that Mr. Cam Douglas was the first person to ever see *her*.

What a strange feeling.

"It's… it's hard to be brave," she admitted as the weight of the wig lifted from her head. She let out a sigh. Then his hands were sifting into her curls, setting them free and scattering the remaining pins. She couldn't help it—now she did lean back into his touch.

"It's the hardest thing most people ever do." He massaged her scalp, and for that alone, she fell a little in love with him. He didn't have to do this. He could throw her down and have his way with her. Instead, he was taking care of her and it was glorious.

"That's why they don't do it. But those who do… " He untied the mask. "Those are the strong ones."

In all the times she had thought about a proper seduction—because she was no angel and she had thought about it—this was not how it had gone. She'd always envisioned flowery language of love and adoration and, yes, beauty.

But this was something entirely different. She wouldn't have guessed that this sort of honest compliment would put her at ease, but that's exactly what it did.

The mask fell away from her face as she exhaled relief. He'd been right—it would be easier without the heavy weight of all the paste diamonds rubbing against her nose.

"Did they tell you what to expect?"

She took a deep breath to make sure her voice was steady when she spoke. "A pinch, a little pain."

He traced the line of her neck before moving down her shoulders, where he stroked over her exposed skin. Little shivers of pleasure coursed through her. "Will you tell me why you need to be ruined? Why you need the money?"

She almost did because somehow, she knew he would understand that her reasons made sense in their own way.

But that was not part of the deal. "I can't."

The buttons at the back of the elaborate dress began to give. It had been too snug in the bosom, despite her tightest corset and the best that the Jewels had been able to do in letting it out. Lady Ruby had insisted that having Cynthia's breasts pushed up this high was a good thing, but oh, how sweet it was to draw a deep breath as the bodice gave.

He made a humming noise as cool air touched her back. If this was seduction, she decided she liked it. She liked it quite a bit.

"Have you been kissed before, my darlin' girl? Had a sweetheart who touched you in a stolen moment? Given your heart to some cad?"

She thought of the few times she'd been cornered—including ones by Beau Haughton. She thought of all the suitors her father had turned away, attractive young men of her station who could've made her a good husband. "I don't think it counts if I didn't want to be kissed, does it?"

His hands stilled, one flat against her spine. "No, it doesn't."

Unexpectedly, he wrapped an arm around her waist and pulled her back into his bare chest. She could feel his skin against hers, warm and sensual and almost too much. That hard, hot length of him—the part of him that he would somehow put inside her—pressed against her hip.

She almost sighed with the pleasure of it. Her! Cynthia Hobbs! Perhaps she was a wanton at heart and just hadn't known it until this very moment.

"Here's what we're going to do," he said, his voice a whisper in her ear. His whiskers scraped over her tender flesh and she had to bite back a moan. "When you're ready, you kiss me. You're in control here. Understood?"

She nodded just as the gown gave and slid down. Her corset wasn't as fancy as some the Jewels had shown her, just a soft peach silk, edged in white lace. But it was pretty enough and oddly, she found herself hoping that he liked it.

She had to kiss him. Before the night was out he would be inside of her and she would be ruined, but somehow, the fact that *she* had to kiss *him* felt monumental.

"So brave," he murmured as he worked the skirt over her hips and then the whole thing fell and she was in nothing but her stays and a shift so fine it was practically transparent. She didn't even have on drawers, just stockings and garters. Lady Ruby had been very clear about that. Jewels did *not* wear drawers.

"Here." His voice was gruff as he stepped to the side and offered her his hand.

She took it, feeling the warmth of his touch, the safety of it. She stepped out of the other woman's dress and turned to face him. She could do this. For just one night, she could be a woman who was equal to this man.

He was down to his smallclothes, which meant that very little separated him from her. "Now what?" she asked.

"Now," he said, bowing over her hand as if they were in a drawing room instead of a bedroom, "I get you a glass of wine."

She nodded, not trusting her voice.

He stepped to the small table where a bottle of red wine that stood next to two stemmed glasses. There was a selection of tiny cakes and cut sandwiches, as well as some cookies. It looked like a tea service, elegant and simple. Cynthia had no idea if this was normal or if Lady Ruby was going above and beyond for her first time. But she appreciated it all the same.

Cam leaned over the table, pouring carefully. There were more scars on his back, including a long one that looked like a knife wound. But they were all healed, nothing recent. His back was strong and powerful and she could see herself running her hands over his skin, feeling his muscles for herself. His legs were hairy, and she could see the outline of his backside. It was scandalous that she was even looking, but she supposed soon enough the thin fabric would be cast aside, so looking now couldn't be any more scandalous than that.

He turned and caught her staring. "Questions?" He held out the glass for her.

She took it and drank deeply while she studied his face. He was a rough man, no doubt, but he was no less handsome for it. His eyes were dark, but his smile was quick and relaxed. She wouldn't like to see him angry, that was certain. But like this? He was completely at ease.

"This isn't going like I thought it would. But," she went on, when his eyebrows jumped up, "I don't think that's a bad thing. In fact," she said, taking a deep breath, "I think it's a good thing."

Oh. He had a dimple when he smiled. "This wasn't how I'd planned on spending the evening, either. But I'm glad you're here with me. I couldn't bear to watch you walk off with one of those two asses."

She took another long drink of wine. It hit her empty stomach in a wave. Already, she could feel it working, her muscles relaxing. Her smile came easier. "I hadn't thought I might actually be able to enjoy this."

"Darlin', I'll make you a promise now—you will like this. If I'm doing it right, you'll like it a whole bunch. Understood?"

His smile sent warmth pouring through her veins and, without being aware of it, her gaze dropped to where his smallclothes were tented.

She was alone with an attractive, kind man who was solicitous of her feelings, who saw her as she really was. It would've been better if this had been her wedding night, but it was good enough for now.

He was right—she had been braced for pain and punishment and humiliation. She had been prepared for a terrible night that would haunt her for the rest of her days. But she was still willing to do it because that was the only way to freedom.

But what if instead this was a night she remembered fondly? A magical night she'd spent with a handsome stranger who made her feel safe and comforted and maybe even very good?

Wouldn't that be worth the price?

Chapter Seven

Cam was not the kind of man who dealt with a lot of conflicted feelings. He robbed stagecoaches for a living and had killed a man or two in his time. He had no trouble sleeping at night. But this was something different. This wasn't armed robbery. And the situation was anything but clear.

For one short second, he wished he were the kind of man who could deal with women the way he dealt with stagecoaches. This Diamond—it was hard to think of her like that, because he knew that wasn't her name—she turned his head right around.

She was a complete innocent, maybe the bravest woman he'd ever had the pleasure of meeting. But she was also temptation in the flesh, her sweet nipples straining at the fabric of her shift, the darker triangle of curls that covered her sex outlined below. He wanted to wrap his arms around her waist and bend her over and plunge into her sweet cunny until he came and then, when he could think again, he wanted to do it a second time.

And a third.

The effort it took not to debauch her straight off was making his arms shake as he ran the bath. But he held himself back. She might say she was here by her choice, but just flipping up her skirts and pounding into her would be little better than rape. The chances were good he was never going to see her again after tonight, but she would think of him. He didn't want those memories to cause her pain.

So it was settled. Seduction first, sex second.

Lady Ruby had thought of everything—there was a fresh cake of fragrant soap next to the bath and lit candles scattered around, giving the room a soft glow.

Diamond had finished her wine when he came back out. She smiled when he took the glass from her and refilled it, a real smile that softened her eyes. God, she was beautiful. Even with her hair a fright from the wig being squashed over her head, even with that shadow of worry dancing at the edges of her smile, she was simply the most perfect woman he'd ever seen. His body burned for her and it was far more than needing a good fuck.

She was his. It didn't make any sense, but he felt it with deep certainty. She was *his* and his alone.

"This is pretty," he said, as he turned her so he could undo the laces of her corset. It was a lame attempt at a compliment but the best he could think of. He had a feeling that if he told her that her tits were the most magnificent pair he'd ever seen, she might get all shy on him again.

"Thank you. It's mine. Nothing else is."

The laces gave and he reached around the front to undo the busks nestled between her breasts. He was more than half hard now, the smell of her skin filling his nose. Lavender, he thought. Something floral and light.

The corset gave. Cam laid it aside—carefully, because it was hers. She stood very still, but he didn't sense the same panic rolling off her. The wine must be working, thank God.

Slowly, he crumpled the shift in his hand and lifted it over her head. Then her back was bare to him, her ass flaring out from her waist. He ran his fingers over her shoulders, down her back, tracing the lines the corset had left on her. She had a mole on her right shoulder and he brushed his fingers over it. "You are lovely," he said. "I hope I'm not the first person to tell you that."

She shook her head. "No, you're not. But it's all anyone ever says to me. As if the fact that I'm pretty is the only thing worthwhile about me."

He didn't miss the bitterness in her voice. "Do you really remember me from the street?"

As he spoke, he rubbed full circles on her shoulders. He desperately wanted to step back and glory in her body, but there would be time enough for that. They had hours. Instead, he pushed her toward the bath. There was a chair next to it—the same chair Ruby had sat on when she had shaved him last time. He sat Diamond on it now and knelt before her, undoing the garters and slowly rolling down the stocking on her right leg.

It took all his restraint to not lean forward and taste her sweetness for himself. He would soon—oh, he would—but he wanted her more relaxed than this. Besides, it wouldn't kill him to have another bath.

When he bared her delicate foot, he traced his fingers over the sole. She giggled, her toes curling around his finger. "That tickles."

"Hmm," he said, turning his attention to her other stocking. His blood was pounding and his cock was rock-hard now, but he focused on her.

Then she was completely nude before him. No one else had ever gotten to see her like this. She was something special and rare and for him alone.

Mine. That was the word that ricocheted around his mind as he skimmed his hands over her calves, past her knees. It took effort to stop at her thighs, but he managed. Her legs were spread just enough that he could glimpse the ruddy pink of her sex beneath her light brown curls.

He slid his hands upward, spreading her thighs even more.

"What are you doing?" she asked in a whisper.

"Admiring the view. My God, you're perfect." He slid his hands around to her ass and pulled her forward on the chair, just enough that he could get a proper look. "What do you call this?" he asked, tracing a finger over her slit and up to her little button. A shiver raced through her and he managed to drag his gaze up to her face.

She had her lower lip tucked under her teeth and a riotous blush darkened her cheeks. "I don't know. My... my sex, I guess. What do you call it?"

"Ah, there are so many names." He spread her lips a bit, exposing the darker red flesh underneath. "Cunt, although that's a rude word. Slit, cunny, quim, pussy... "

"Is cunny bad?"

"Not if you like it." He stroked his fingers over her again, watching the shiver as it moved over her body. God, she would be amazing—responsive and sensitive.

Mine.

"It rhymes with honey."

"That it does." He could see her body responding, that little button growing slicker as he petted her. "I've heard it called a honeypot, too."

"Really?" He glanced up, amused by her incredulous tone. "Why?"

"Because when you want a man, you grow wet for him. Like this." He ran his finger around her button, feeling her desire rising. "Makes it easier to take a man into you, when you're slick and relaxed and wanting him." He dipped his finger down, sliding just the tip of a finger into her. "Here. Here's where I'm going to put my cock into you and ruin you."

She made a whimpering noise of need high in the back of her throat.

"Do you know why they say that? Why they call loving a man a woman's ruin?"

"Because," she answered breathlessly, her legs beginning to twitch as her need built. "A woman's value is her virginity. Without it, she's ruined. She's nothing."

He almost pulled up short at that. Is that how she saw herself? After tonight, she'd be a nothing? A lie, that. She'd be so much more by the time he left her. She'd be a woman who knew her power and wasn't afraid of it.

He *tsked*, then slid his finger in again. A little farther this time. Her muscles clenched tight around him, pushing back at the invasion. "Some see it that way," he said, his voice straining as he fought for control. God, to see her body take him in. He leaned his head to the side, scraping his stubble over the sensitive skin of her inner thigh. "But the truth is that, after I take you, you'll always compare any other man

71

to me and always find them wanting. *That's* what being ruined is."

But even as he said it, he wondered if the reverse weren't true. What if she ruined him?

"Are you—*oh*," she squeaked when he added his thumb back to her little button, "are you that—that good?"

"Darlin', I'm better." He pulled free of her. She made a little mewling noise as he held up his finger. "See? See how your sweet honey is all over my finger?"

He waited while she looked her fill, her hands gripping the sides of the chair, her generous tits heaving with hard, short little pants. "Yes."

He licked her honey off his finger, savoring the tang and the sweetness of her. She gasped, her hips lifting toward him. Her scent filled his nose, her taste coated his tongue—oh yeah, he was going to bury his face between her thighs and lick her until she screamed.

"I thought you weren't going to do anything until I kissed you," she said, her voice high and tight with need as she shifted on the chair. She might not know what she wanted, but by God her body did.

"This?" He grinned at her, spreading her wide with his fingertips. She moaned, a quiet noise that she tried to hold inside. "This isn't hardly anything, darlin'. This is just an education. You've got your cunny—and a pretty one it is, soft and pink and delicate," he told her as he stroked against her flesh. "And then up here, you've got your clit. Some call it their button or pearl or nub, but nub isn't a sweet enough word for this little beauty."

"I... oh, God," she moaned as it came to life under Cam's touch. "I didn't know."

"It's okay," he said, stroking her body and slipping that lucky finger back inside of her. Didn't make a damn bit of sense to him why society deemed that girls shouldn't even know how their own bodies worked. Seemed cruel to set a girl up for a lifetime of not getting what she needed in bed in the name of protecting her virtue.

He could give her this. Someone had once told him that knowledge was power. He could give her a good memory of her first time and the knowledge to make sure she always got the sex she deserved. "Which word did you like?"

"Pearl," she gasped as his finger slid in a little farther, to the second knuckle. "Is this... " She gulped, trying to get herself under control. "Is this how we do this?"

He withdrew and she made that little mewling sound again. "There's no one way, my darlin' girl. And it's going to hurt at first, just a little." He didn't want to lie to her. He could work a finger and then maybe two into her, but she was tight around his finger, and his cock was a hell of a lot more to take in.

He stood and plucked at the string of his smallclothes. "But just tell me to stop or wait or we'll try something else, okay?"

"How bad will it hurt?" Her voice wavered. But even as she asked, she sat up and squared her shoulders, ready to battle.

"Not too much. I'll do my best to be gentle with you." Which was more than she would have gotten with anyone else in that saloon tonight.

He worked his drawers down over his throbbing erection. Her eyes went huge at the sight of him, but she didn't look away, God bless her.

He fisted his hand around his shaft and stroked up, then down. Her gaze followed the movement and then her tongue slipped out, tracing a path along her lips and he remembered that she hadn't kissed him yet, hadn't made that choice.

Soon, though. She would soon or he'd die on the spot.

"I'm going to touch you and pet you and kiss your cunny, your precious little pearl until you shatter with lust," he promised her as he stroked himself for her. "I'm going to make you so happy and then, when you're wet and ready for me, I'll take you." Her brow knit with worry and he cast about for something that would reassure her. "It's like... like shoes."

She blinked at him. "Shoes?"

"Yeah," he said, letting go of his aching cock and pulling her to her feet. Her body was warm against his, the tips of her tits grazing his chest. The head of his cock brushed against her belly, soft and inviting. He settled his hands around her waist and then lifted.

"Cam!" she squealed, throwing her arms around his neck as he set her in the tub.

"Shoes," he said, hanging onto his self-control by his fingernails. "You ever buy a pair of boots or shoes or whatever you fine ladies wear, and the leather was stiff? So the first time, maybe your toes pinch or you get a blister or whatever. But they're nice shoes so you wear them again and the next time's not so bad and before you know it, you've broken them in and they're like a part of you?"

74

She leaned back, a small smile on her face. Thank God. "Just so I understand you correctly, I'm the boot in this analogy and you—*this*," she said, pointedly looking down at his throbbing cock, "is the foot?"

"It's not a perfect example," he grumbled good-naturedly, which made her smile. Then he climbed into the tub with her and sat, the hot water sluicing over his thighs and his cock bobbing to the surface.

She stood, apparently unaware of exactly how much Cam could see at this angle. Her pretty cunny, the generous swell of her breasts, the tips pointing almost straight out. He reached up and stroked her calf. "I already had a bath today," she said quietly. "Before I got dressed up."

"Ah, but I haven't and I want to come to you fresh as a daisy," he said, grabbing the soap and a cloth and sudsing it up. He scrubbed his face and neck, then his chest and arms, and finally his legs while she watched, letting her get familiar with his body. Then he swiped the cloth over his cock, making the damn thing twitch. He was doing the best he could but how much longer could he hold out?

"If I have a cunny and a pearl," she said, her mouth moving daintily over the words, "then what do you have?"

"A cock. This," he said, fisting himself and pushing his hips out of the water so she could see better, "is the head. It loves nothing more than a good kiss and a sweet cunny." He glanced up at her. She was practically scarlet with a blush that covered her whole body, but she didn't hide her face.

"A kiss?"

"Yeah," he said, his voice gruff as he pictured her

bending over him, her pink lips wrapping around his cock for a kiss. "And this, the long part? That's the shaft. You grip it good and tight, like this," he said, demonstrating for her, "and slide your hands up and down. Underneath, those are my stones. I like to have them cupped—but gently, like you were handling an egg."

He reached between his legs and fondled his stones, feeling them tighten as she stared, her mouth open in a perfect little *O* as he pleasured himself for her. Unexpectedly, she sat on the edge of the tub, looking more than a little dizzy with lust.

If nothing else, this was highly educational.

It was also pure torture. He kept his movements slow, gritting his teeth against the climax that begged to be unleashed. He wanted to pull her down onto him, thrust up into her tight cunny and claim her as his. No one else's, just *his*.

He did no such thing. Instead, he forced himself to let go of his aching cock and take up the soap and cloth again. He held it out to her and, when she took it, he turned his back to her and waited.

Close to a minute passed before the water shifted. She knelt and began to scrub him, her touch light. "This is scandalous," she murmured as she stroked his skin.

"Darlin', I haven't yet begun to scandalize you." The cloth moved over his shoulders.

"Are you like this with all your women?"

He snorted. Oh yeah, the wine was working. "First off, I don't have *that* many women. And second off, no, not quite like this. I've never bedded a virgin before, so I want to make sure we do it right. Women of considerable experience don't always require such... preparation."

"Because the boot's already been broken in?"

"Exactly." He chuckled and was pleased to hear her laugh with him. He leaned forward, almost draped over the side of the tub to expose his lower back and his ass. Would she touch him? "Tell me about some things you like." Because if she was talking, she wasn't thinking. And thinking was bad right now.

"Oh, I suppose I like to do all those vain and silly things that young ladies too. I like pretty dresses. And hats and shoes and shawls. I learned how to knit just because I saw a shawl I liked once." She stroked lower over his back and he had to clench his fists to keep from rolling over and pulling her on top of him.

"I can play the piano, but I'm not very good at it," she went on. "And I enjoy reading. I read out loud to—" She broke off, suddenly silent. Worse, though, was the way the cloth stopped rubbing over his skin.

"What kind of stories?"

Something touched his ass—but it wasn't fabric. It was her fingertips, taking his measure. He held absolutely still.

"Fairy tales," she said in a small voice, as if she should be ashamed of that. "All those old stories, the *Knights of the Round Table, Hansel and Gretel, Robin Hood*—that's one of my favorites."

Something flared in his chest. She liked an outlaw, did she? "Robin Hood is one of my favorites, too," he managed to say through gritted teeth as she palmed his ass. "That feels good."

She stilled against him. "Is it... is it all right?"

He barked out a laugh. "Darlin' girl, I'm yours.

77

Touch me, ask questions—whatever you want is mighty fine by me." Then he waited.

Would she touch him?

"Cam?" Her hands slid to his side, then began to move to the front, where his aching cock stood stiff at attention.

"Yeah, darlin'?" Then he groaned as she leaned into him, her breasts pressing against his back, her hands circling his cock. He almost shot his load right then and there. "God," he breathed, fighting the urge to thrust into her hands.

He groaned as she gripped him and pulled, just like he'd shown her.

"I'm glad you won me."

Chapter Eight

This was insane, that's what it was.

She was sprawled against Cam's naked back, her arms wrapped around his waist, his... his *cock* firmly in her hands. She was touching it, so she might as well be able to say the correct name.

Even though the water was still quite warm, she could feel the heat coming off him as she stroked up and down, just like she'd seen him do. He was long and hard in her hands, strong and soft at the same time. How... curious.

"That's it," he said, his voice a harsh whisper. "That's it, my darlin' girl." With that, his hips begin to move, pushing into her hands and then pulling back. She held on tight as a low groan broke free of him. "God, that's good."

Insane, yes. But there was still something powerful about this moment. She was doing it right— but more than that, she had this big, strong man reduced to practically begging.

Her! A virgin!

He'd said that when she was ready for him, she would grow wet with her own honey. She could feel that happening, feel a warm heaviness building between her thighs. It was unlike anything she'd felt before, throbbing and insistent, and somehow she knew Cam was the only person who could make it all better.

"Oh God, *yes*," he groaned as she tightened her grip around the shaft of his cock. "This is how your cunny will hold me, sweetheart. And this," he said, thrusting his hips forward, "is how I'll move in you. This is how men and women fuck."

She gasped at the curse words, her body tightening almost to the point of pain.

"Yeah," he said, his back arching with another thrust. "This is how I'm going to fuck you. Slow and steady and hard until you're begging me for more, until you come for me. Do you want that, sweetheart? Do you want to come with my thick cock buried inside you?"

Cynthia was already ruined. He'd already been inside of her, even if it was just his wicked finger. The deal had been sealed and now? Now she wanted to know *everything*. Isn't that what some of the girls had told her? There might be a little pinch at the beginning, but then it was worth it? When it was good, it was so, *so* good? She wanted good. She wanted him to fuck her, wanted to feel that flying bliss break over her again like it had in her dreams.

And only he could give it to her.

So she leaned forward and pressed her lips against a scar on his back and hoped that this was the right thing, hoped that when he was done putting his cock inside her, she would be able to go on without him.

The next thing she knew, he'd spun in her arms, splashing water everywhere. "Cam!" she squeaked as he grabbed her by the waist and pulled. It seemed only natural for her legs to spread as he hauled her over his chest, her knees coming to rest on either side of his hips.

And then he was against her, that thick, hard cock that she had been touching pressed against her pearl.

She hadn't even known she'd had a pearl, for Pete's sake. But she did and it had come alive under his fingers. She wanted him to go back to touching it or—he had said something about *kissing* it, hadn't he?

"Are you sure?" But even as he spoke, his hips continued to move, dragging his cock against her sex, against her pearl and the opening to her cunny. Her cheeks flamed at the thought, at all of it.

She liked him. Handsome and strong and kind and gentle and patient. And *hers*. He was more than she'd thought she'd get. "I'm sure." Breathing hard, she buried her fingers into his jet-black hair and tilted his face up. His hands were at her waist, his fingertips digging into her hips. But he didn't move. He just sat there and waited for her. She closed the distance between them and pressed her lips against his.

This was her first kiss. Her first real kiss with a real man, not some forced touch that made her feel ashamed and dirty. His lips were soft, although the stubble on his face pricked at her cheeks. But...

She pulled back, frowning. Where was the heat that sent her senses spiraling? Where was the desire that made her weak?

"Did I do it wrong?" she asked, embarrassment rising fast.

A knowing grin on his face, he let go of her, his hands going to the side of the tub. "It was sweet, wasn't it?"

Without being aware of it, she shifted her hips and then gasped when her pearl hit the head of his cock. "Yes, I guess. But I didn't... I don't... " She exhaled in frustration. "Maybe I don't want sweet right now."

"That's my girl," he said and then he was moving, surging out of the tub. Water went everywhere, but she couldn't care. "Wrap your legs around me," he said in her ear, one arm coming underneath her bottom, the other at her back. "Hold on tight."

She nodded into his shoulder and then pressed her lips against his collarbone. Cam made a low growling noise, almost animal in nature, so she did it again. She couldn't imagine doing any of this with Vincent Brown. Just the thought made her shudder, so she pushed it away and focused on Cam Douglas instead, on the powerful movement of his muscles as he carried her. On the way he called her *darling* and *sweetheart* and taught her naughty words under the guise of education.

She could feel his cock bobbing against her as she clung to him, their skin making wet noises as he moved. She let go of her worry. She would take the pain as it came, but it wouldn't be more than she could bear. It would be worth it, to have this man, to be ruined by him for anyone else.

He carried her to the bed and slowly set her down. Then he gently cupped her cheek, stroking his thumb over her skin. She shivered.

"Now," he said, his eyes so dark they were almost black, "*now* we begin." He bent over her and took her mouth.

Oh. *Oh!* He sank one hand into her hair and tilted her head to the side, his mouth slanted over hers. He kissed her as if he'd die without the touch of her lips, as if she might, too. The heat of his touch was burning her from the inside out, her desire spiraling. She moaned into him as his teeth nipped at her lower lip and when she opened for him, his tongue dipped inside her mouth. It was all Cynthia could do to hang on to the bedclothes.

He pulled on her hair, gently forcing her back onto the bed. He raised himself over her, edging her legs apart with his knee. This was it. The moment of truth. She took a deep breath.

Except it wasn't. He sat back and grabbed a towel and stroked the thick cloth over her prone body. He abraded her nipples with it, making them tighten in a way that echoed in her pearl. In a way she didn't understand, but she knew she needed more. Something much, much more. Like something out of a dream, sweet and perfect.

Then the towel dipped between her legs, scraping over her thighs. She shifted her legs apart even more, giving him room to work. The towel moved down, drying her knees and then her feet, and she giggled in frustration. "Cam," she warned, and then she boldly lifted her foot out of his hand and nudged his cock with it. "*Please.*"

He made a deep rumbling noise, not quite a growl but not quite a moan. "So damned polite," he practically snarled. Then he grabbed her by the hips and jerked her to the edge of the bed. The next thing she knew, he knelt between her open legs and his hands were on her cunny again, pulling her apart. Opening her for him. "Not yet, " he said, his voice tight. "I want to make sure you're ready."

A strange whimpering noise filled her ears and it took a moment to realize that she was the one making that noise, desperate and needy. But before she could even feel ashamed, he lowered his mouth and pressed a kiss against her pearl.

She barely had time to gasp as the sensations overwhelmed her before he did it again. This time the stubble on his cheeks scraped over her tender flesh and she writhed underneath him, fisting her hands in the bedclothes. But it wasn't enough. She reached for him, trying to grab hold and get him to do something, she didn't know what. All she could do was sink her fingers into his hair and hold on.

He made a rumbling noise again, right against her skin and she moaned from the pleasure of it. She hadn't known. She'd had *no* idea that this went on between men and women.

He pulled away and she whimpered, knowing it was undignified, but she was helpless to stop. He lifted her legs so they rested over his shoulders and then pulled her closer, anchoring her with one hand across her hips. His thumb came to rest on her curls and he began to burrow for her pearl.

The other hand? He reached up and took hold of her left breast, pulling on her nipple.

Cynthia shoved one hand in her mouth, trying to fight back the cries of pleasure as wave after wave of ecstasy washed over her. His thumb danced over the top of her pearl and his mouth was against her cunny, his tongue doing the most dangerously scandalous things she'd never even imagined were possible. His other hand tugged at her nipple, pulling in rhythm with his thumb and his tongue. He sucked her little pearl between his teeth, the barest pressure making her cry out again. And then he pushed his fingers into her cunny and stroked until she let out a sob that was a noise of pure relief.

Her body was no longer in her control. She was shaking and moaning and crying out, on the edge of something important, something vital to her very survival.

This was being properly *ruined*.

Then it broke over her, that wave of pleasure, and her back came off the bed, her fingers pulling hard on Cam's hair. For a beautiful moment frozen in time, she was nothing but satisfaction and heat, light and happiness.

Then she fell back, shaking, breathing hard. Cam nipped at the delicate skin on her inner thigh and she managed to lift her head to find him staring at her with his dark eyes. The need she saw there was so fierce it took her breath away.

"The sweetest honey," he murmured, pressing another kiss against her pearl before surging to his feet.

All Cynthia could do was watch as he fished something long and pale colored out of a small box on the table beside the bed. He fitted it over his cock—the sheath, she realized.

Then he turned to her, swinging her legs around so that she was laid out on the bed properly. She had a moment to wonder how on earth he was going to fit *that* inside of her and then his body covered hers. The hair on his chest chafed at her sensitive nipples as he kissed her hard, his tongue slipping into her mouth. She tasted her honey, tasted him and her together. And maybe it was wanton and scandalous, but she couldn't help but think they tasted *so* good.

"I can't wait, " he said, pushing back on one arm and holding the head of his sheathed cock against her. "I'll be gentle, my darlin' girl, I promise." He rubbed against her and she could feel her honey spreading over him, that languid heat building again. Then he shifted, pressing against the opening of her cunny. "Hold on to me," he ordered, his voice raw and his arms shaking. "Hold on and don't let go."

He began to thrust. She felt her body open to him and then a wash of pain caused her to gasp. "Cam," she whispered, squeezing her eyes shut tight against the pinpricks of tears.

"Easy," he said, stopping. He shifted, spreading her legs wider and looping one of her knees over his elbow. It opened her even more and she could feel him throbbing against her. "Tell me your name."

"What?" Her eyes flew open and she stared at him in confusion.

He shifted, settling inside of her a little more. When she winced, he said, "Your name, my darlin' girl."

"Why?" Why would he ask right now? *Now* seemed to be a particularly important time she'd like to focus on something besides her name.

He gained another half-inch, an inch—she didn't know. His smile was lazy, as if he had infinite patience. "So when I cry out my pleasure," he said, his hips flexing and driving him deeper inside, "I call out the right name."

She blinked at him. "You would do that?"

But as she spoke, he thrust against her and the pain was sharper. She gasped and tried to push him off, but he held her down, pinned with his weight, his cock fully inside of her. "It hurts," she whimpered, tears leaking out of the sides of her eyes.

"I'm sorry, I'm so sorry," he whispered, kissing away her tears. He stroked her lips with his mouth, his tongue, whispering sweet words of how brave she was, how strong she was—how good she felt, tight around him, how good she tasted under his tongue, crying out her pleasure. And all the while, he held very still inside her.

Then the strangest thing happened—after a moment or two, the burning subsided. She could feel herself stretching around him, feel herself adjusting to this new part in her.

He could feel it, too. He leaned back, smiling down at her. "There. Better?"

Blushing was pointless at this stage, but that didn't stop her cheeks from heating. "A little." She cupped his cheek, stroking the stubble on his skin. The longer he held still, the better she felt. She still couldn't see how this would lead to the same sort of earth-shattering pleasure he'd given her with his mouth, but it wasn't bad.

"So brave." He kissed her again and this time, she felt his hips shift. He moved inside of her and that was a completely new sensation, the push and pull of him. The same push and pull he'd shown her in the tub. He did it a few times and then paused again. "Okay?"

If it was possible to fall in love with a stranger, she might have just done so. No one else would've been this solicitous of her feelings. No one else would have taken his time to make sure she was ready, to give her pleasure first.

Anyone else—including Vincent Brown—

would've thrown her down and poked their way in and not given a Goddamn if she'd hurt. Not a single Goddamn.

No one except this man.

She raked her fingers through his hair and pulled him down. "Cynthia."

His eyes widened and then he fell upon her like a man possessed. His mouth crashed down onto her as he began to thrust with long strokes, strokes she felt through every part of her body. There was little more than a pinch now, already fading, being replaced with that shaking need. She could feel the wave of pleasure rebuilding, feel it pushing against her, making her lift her hips to meet his thrusts, making her whimper with want.

Then he shifted to reach between them and pressed his thumb against her pearl. Suddenly, she was flying again, flying while he held her against the bed, his hips pumping into her, her name on his lips.

"Cynthia—Cynthia!" He cried out as another wave of pleasure, stronger than the first, broke over her. Then he collapsed against her, their chests heaving. It took all of her remaining strength to wrap her arms around him, to hold him tight even as he crushed her.

"Next time," he said, his breath hot against her ear, "it'll be better. It won't hurt, I promise."

Better than that? She started giggling even as he rolled off of her, pulling free. She winced and only then realized that there were still tears trickling down the sides of her face. He propped himself up on his elbow and looked at her, concerned. "Was it too much?"

It wasn't dignified and it most certainly wasn't ladylike, but Cynthia threw herself at him, wrapping her arms around him and slinging a leg over his hip and burying her face against his chest. "It was wonderful," she said, feeling a strange sort of lightness. "I'm so glad it was you."

He made that rumbling noise of happiness again as he flopped onto his back and pulled her, half sprawled, on top of him. They lay like that for a long time, until the sweat began to cool on her back and she shivered. He sat up, kissing her quick and hard. She couldn't help but stare at his cock, which was now considerably smaller than it'd been just a few minutes ago and lying limply inside the sheath.

Men were very strange creatures, she decided.

He lifted her chin, making her look him in the eyes. "We have to get cleaned up, but then I'll hold you for as long as I can, all right?"

A strange, lonely sort of sadness gripped her. Oh, if only he could hold onto her. If only this had been her wedding night instead of an act borne of desperation and fear. She couldn't change things, though. Lady Ruby had been right—there was no undoing this and there was most certainly no room for what-ifs.

So Cynthia did what she had to do. She squared her shoulders as she slipped out of bed, wincing at her newly tender parts. Because as much as she might have fallen in love with him and as good as he'd made her feel, she knew the truth of the matter.

After tonight, she would never see him again.

Chapter Nine

What had he done?

Cam took care of the sheath and then splashed cold water on his face. The whole time, his head swam with the question.

Jesus Christ, what had he *done*?

It'd seemed so straightforward. Use the Jeweled Ladies to establish his alibi and get a hot bath and sex out of it. It'd been a good plan, a simple one.

At the exact moment he'd recognized the proud set of Cynthia's shoulders, the plan had gone right the hell out the window and he'd come up with a new plan on the spot. Protect an innocent from lecherous old bastards. Introduce her—slowly, carefully—to the joys of sex. And then walk away, his alibi firmly in place.

He was always able to walk away. Sex was a release—fun, easy, good. Right up there with a nice whiskey and a great meal. Nothing more, nothing less. Something he enjoyed and then forgot about by the next day.

How in the holy hell was he supposed to walk away from her now? Because he knew he'd never forget this night. Never forget her. In a way he didn't completely understand, she'd always be his. And in a perfect world, he'd always be hers. He wasn't supposed to feel anything, dammit. Not for her.

But he did. In all honesty, he had from the very first moment he'd touched her, back in the street.

Hell.

He looked at himself in the huge mirror behind Ruby's washstand and for the first time, he wondered about the man looking back at him. He was a stagecoach robber who paid for a woman when he needed one, but he had some morals, damn it. A code of honor—honor among thieves, but honor all the same. He tried his damnedest not to kill anyone and never left anyone for dead. He'd saved Hatfield's life and made the boy his partner. He made sure any dove he fucked was both well satisfied and well paid. Hell, he'd risked his life to make sure that mother and daughter hadn't been taken prisoner by the Comanche, for God's sake. He might not be Robin Hood but he was a good enough man.

Now? He'd debauched a young woman and he was just going to—to what? To walk away from her? To abandon her to whatever fate she was trying so damned hard to escape? For what? So he could go rob a bank right out from underneath another criminal?

God, he wished he were a better man. One who already had a piece of land and his horses and some cattle, who had enough to give someone as sweet and brave as Cynthia everything she needed and protect her from the cruelties of this world.

Nothing about this felt honorable. Instead, he felt… wrong. Dirty, despite the bath.

When he walked back into the bedroom, Cynthia was curled on her side, watching him through lidded eyes. Her gaze swept over him and unconsciously, he straightened up and thrust out his chest. But even that made him feel dirty again. "Are you really sixteen?"

he asked, hoping that, like her hair and her name, her age had been a lie.

"Twenty." She tried to hide a yawn behind her hand, but failed. "Lady Ruby wanted me to seem more virginal, I guess. Plus, saying my real age would make it easier for someone to figure out who I was." She scooted over, making room for him in the bed.

"Twenty is a good age," he told her, relieved beyond measure. She was a grown woman, then—not a child. Thank God for that. "Here. Let me hold you."

If she were any other woman in this brothel, Cam would roll her onto her stomach and take her from behind. Or maybe he'd pull her on top and watch her tits bounce as he thrust up into her—didn't matter, as long as he was buried inside of her. But he knew that she'd be sore. And besides, his head was a mess with these unfamiliar emotions. Damn his protective instincts.

Those instincts had to be why he said, "You listen to me, Miss Cynthia," as he tucked in beside her, wrapping his arm around her shoulders and pulling her against his chest.

"Oh?" She sounded sleepy and happy as she snuggled against his side.

God, but she felt right there. She fit against him, just like he'd fit inside her. And yet, he was going to walk away in a few short hours. Fool that he was.

"Now you know what you need," he said, trying to find the words that would make sense to her. "Before you do anything crazy like marry someone, you make sure that he'll treat you right in bed and out of it. Make sure he listens to you and does what you want. You make sure he has a care for your feelings and puts your pleasure first, you hear? Promise me that."

He could feel the wave of tension ripple over her body and then her arms tightened around his waist. "I might never marry," she warned. "I think I've been ruined for all other men. How could they live up to you?"

He kissed the top of her head and stroked her back and tried not to think about this gorgeous, vibrant woman being alone for the rest of her days. "Just promise me, my darlin' girl."

"I promise." Her voice was solemn and he knew she meant it. Good. If nothing else—nothing beside the money, that was—at the very least he'd given her this.

Eventually, she slept. She probably wasn't used to late hours, after all. Cam held her the whole time as she dreamed. He dreamt with her, but he was awake. If he didn't get himself killed in a few hours, he'd have close to five thousand dollars to his name. Maybe he'd go back up to Missouri. His mother's people were still scattered in the Ozark Mountains and they might welcome him home. But even if they didn't, he knew the land. It wasn't much good for farming.

But raising horses? Ranch hands liked quarter horses for their cattle work, but Cam knew Missouri Fox Trotters. Their smooth trot would make them an easy sell to cowboys who spent their days in the saddle and Trotters had the temperament for dealing with cattle.

He smiled to himself. After all these years, he might finally do what his father had wanted him to do in the first place—settle down and breed horses. Too bad the old man wasn't alive to see it come to pass.

Five thousand dollars could buy him a nice piece of land, a comfortable house, some mares and a stud. He could set himself up as a gentleman breeder, far away from the First Macon County Bank and Brimstone, Texas.

Cam looked down at the woman sleeping in his arms. Would it be enough for her? Could *he* be enough for her? Would she even want him, if she knew the truth? She was clearly an honorable woman, despite the virgin auction. Maybe she only wanted a memory, not a lifetime.

He scoffed quietly at himself. Even if he managed to rob the bank and make it back to Missouri and set himself up on a ranch with a comfortable house and a herd of Fox Trotters, how would he ever find her again? The list of things he knew about her was short. Her name was Cynthia. She was twenty years old. She had curly blonde hair and an iron will. She was no longer a virgin. And she had great tits. That was it. He didn't think she'd still be in Brimstone this time next week and he didn't have a lot of faith that Lady Ruby would forward Cynthia a letter from Cam.

Didn't matter. He wasn't going to retire from stagecoach robbing for her. He was going to do it for himself and Hatfield, if the boy wanted to come along. If they pooled their money, they'd be able to afford half of Taney County.

Just before two, he slipped out of bed. He wished he could wake her up with a kiss that would become something much more, but it wasn't meant to be. He couldn't risk contacting Lady Ruby in the future because, despite his excellent alibi, he'd be a suspect in the bank robbery. No, he was leaving Brimstone and not looking back until he was well clear of Texas.

Quietly, he dressed. He couldn't resist one last look at Cynthia. He leaned over the bed and smoothed her curls away from her face and then kissed her forehead. "I'll never forget you," he whispered. "Be strong, my darlin' girl."

Then he walked out the door.

Mr. Steel, the big man who'd acted as a bodyguard, was sitting in a chair a little way down the hall, whittling. He looked up as Cam closed the door behind him. "She's asleep," he said, keeping his voice quiet. The whole brothel was quiet. He'd been in this place when laughter and cries of delight rang out of seemingly every corner, but now there were only faint murmurs floating down the hallway, ghosts of pleasure.

The big man notched an eyebrow at Cam and ran his knife down the piece of wood again, peeling off a long, perfect curl.

Cam fought the urge to roll his eyes. Another silent fellow. Was it Cam? It wasn't like he went looking for men who didn't talk. They just found him, it seemed.

If this guy thought Cam could be intimidated, he was in for a hell of a surprise. "I had a friend— Hatfield? Do you know where he is?"

The big man eyed him suspiciously and then nodded once. He stood and led Cam down the front stairs.

Cam was somewhat surprised to see Hatfield back in the parlor. This time, instead of perching on a pink chair and looking like he wanted to bolt, the boy was on a settee, holding hands with the young woman in the pretty purple dress. Her hair was down now and Hatfield looked clean and shiny and only slightly embarrassed when Cam walked into the room.

"There you are," Cam said. He bowed to the girl. "Did you have a good night, Miss Amethyst?"

She beamed, her cheeks pinking. "I enjoyed spending the evening with your friend."

Hatfield stood and the girl stood with him. It was cute, the way they clung to each other's hands. In a different life, it would've looked like a young pup courting his first love instead of a boy paying for his first whore. Cam felt a twinge of guilt. He liked Hatfield. They made a good team. But maybe he should've tried harder to keep the kid away from a life of crime.

This was not the time for reflection and second-guessing. They had a bank to rob, for Christ's sake.

He didn't like the fact that there was an audience for their departure from the Jeweled Ladies. At least the big guy probably wouldn't tell on them, but he didn't know about the girl. And Cynthia, well, she was safely asleep.

"Miss Amethyst," he said, with an exaggerated bow to the girl, "thank you for your time tonight. I'm sure it has been Hatfield's greatest honor." He winked because he knew it would piss the boy off.

True enough, Hatfield scowled at him. Then he leaned over and kissed the girl's cheek. She smiled prettily and put her hand on his chest, as if she wanted to hold onto him.

"I hope to see you again," she said. Which was sweet, but also what all of the Jewels said at the end of the night.

Hatfield opened his mouth and almost said something. Cam's jaw about hit the floor—the boy spoke so rarely. But then the kid realized that Cam was staring so instead he leaned in and kissed the girl's cheek again before he let go of her hand.

Cam turned and caught the way Mr. Steel was staring at Hatfield with something that looked like shock. Cam didn't like that. He didn't want anyone to be able to describe either of them.

Of course, if that were the case, he probably shouldn't have outbid the mayor for the right to deflower a virgin. Safe to say that Hatfield was not being the memorable one here.

A flash of scarlet caught the corner of his eye and then he was face-to-face with Lady Ruby. "Well?" she said, slipping her hand through his arm. She was still wearing the same blood-red dress, not a hair out of place. Only the slight divot between her eyebrows gave away her worry.

"I did right by her," he replied, leading her out to the entryway. Hatfield trailed after them, but Mr. Steel and Amethyst stayed in the parlor. "She'll be sore in the morning but she'll have good memories—and there won't be a child."

Lady Ruby patted his cheek. "Thank you, Cam. You are a scoundrel and a rogue but you might just be a gentleman after all." She tilted her head and gave him a real smile. "I don't think I'd want you any other way."

He grinned at her. Yeah, they were equals, him and Ruby. "You'll take care of her, won't you? I assume she's leaving town tomorrow. You'll make sure she gets safely away?"

Lady Ruby's eyes crinkled at the corners and Cam thought she looked pleased. "Of course, that was the deal. She'll be gone before anyone misses her. I give you my word."

Cam caught up her hand and pressed a kiss to the back of it. "I don't think I'll be seeing you again, my lady. But it has been an honor to know you."

"Likewise, Mr. Douglas. And if you do find

yourself back in this part of the country, stop in and see me. My door will always be open to you."

He headed out but then pulled up short on the stoop. "Oh—I need to pay for Hatfield's time."

Lady Ruby stood in the doorway, light streaming out behind her. She looked like an angel, one that hadn't needed to avenge anyone tonight, thank God. "It's on the house—with my thanks, Cam." With that, she shut the door.

Damn, he was going to miss that woman. But not as much as he'd miss Cynthia, whoever she was. God, he felt like a cad leaving her. But that was the deal, wasn't it? One night. Nothing more and not a damned thing less.

Cam turned to Hatfield. "Did you have a nice time?"

The boy shifted his mouth, like he was going to spit but was clean out of tobacco.

Cam snorted. "Yeah, yeah. We've got work to do. Seeing as I spent all of our money on a virgin." He made it a policy not to lie to his partner.

Instead of stabbing him, however, Hatfield just gave him a dull look.

"Hey—you heard how grateful Lady Ruby was," Cam defended. "That girl needed me. I couldn't just leave her to those lecherous bastards."

Hatfield held his gaze, a challenge in his eyes.

"Don't give me that look. You got a woman out of it, too. And the five hundred is coming out of my share of this job, okay?"

Hatfield rolled his eyes and slunk off into the shadows.

Right. They had a bank to rob.

Chapter Ten

S issy?"

Exhausted, Cynthia forced her eyes open. The wagon she and Sarah were riding in the back of had rocked her into a daze, one in which Cam's mouth did wicked, wicked things to her. "What is it, sweetie?"

Sarah was curled up against Cynthia's side, a light blanket thrown over them and their carpetbags acting as pillows. Thank goodness it wasn't winter.

This was not how Cynthia normally travelled. This farmer's wagon had no cushioning and she felt every bump and rut in her bones. To say nothing of the lingering smell of sheep, and other things she didn't want to even think about. But Lady Ruby had insisted they take a wagon out of town. A carriage would've been too noticeable.

"I'm sad," Sarah said and then she began to make little whimpering noises.

Cynthia sighed. She was tired and sore—although not in a bad way. Every jostle reminded her that just a few hours before, Cam had made love to her.

They hit another rut and she winced. She supposed she was thankful for the wagon. If Lady Ruby had told her she'd had to ride a horse out of Brimstone, Cynthia might've broken down and cried.

It had been worth it though. Cam Douglas had been *worth* it.

"Why are you sad?" she asked, keeping her tone light.

"My hair is sad," Sarah said, beginning to sniffle.

Oh dear. If she didn't get Sarah calmed down right now, the girl would launch herself into a full-fledged tantrum. "Sweetie, we talked about this," Cynthia said, stroking over her sister's newly shorn hair. "Hair grows back. And when we get to where we're going, I'll help you fix it so it looks real pretty."

Lady Ruby had insisted that Sarah be transformed into Sam. They hadn't been able to convince Sarah to wear a cloth binding her breasts down, but they did have her in a loose linen shirt with a thick vest buttoned up tight and a jacket thrown over that.

The jewel Garnet, the one who had affixed the wig to Cynthia's head, had also cut Sarah's hair in a rough bob that came almost to her shoulders. Sarah's hair was not as curly as Cynthia's, but had a definite wave to it. Cynthia had been so proud of her sister when she had not thrown a tantrum during the haircut. Mostly it had been because she was too excited about wearing trousers. Who knew her sister would enjoy trousers?

"Sissy?"

Cynthia smiled. She honestly wasn't sure Sarah knew her real name. She hadn't been able to pronounce *Cynthia* as a child. Cynthia had always been Sissy. "Yes, sweetheart?"

"My name is sad, too."

Cynthia bit back a laugh as she looked up at the stars. "You're only Sam for a little bit. As soon as we get where we're going, you're going to go right back to being Sarah, the happiest girl I know."

Sarah hummed at the thought of being the happiest girl in the world. But then she asked, "Where are we going?"

Well, that was the question, wasn't it? "We're headed for Kansas City," Cynthia said, sounding more confident than she felt. Cynthia had two hundred and fifty dollars and two train tickets from McKinney to Kansas City. But she had no idea where they were going from there.

There would be time to figure that out. They had enough money to live on for a year, maybe more if Cynthia was careful. But it wasn't as if she could go out and get a job. Aside from caring for Sarah, she had no other skills and she couldn't leave Sarah alone all day.

First things first. A black man named Donald Shane was driving them to McKinney, which was a little more than fifty miles from Brimstone. Mr. Shane was keeping the two horses at a steady trot. The lantern hanging off the side of the wagon swung wildly, casting long shadows over what passed for a road around here. She wished they could go faster, but it just wasn't safe in the dark.

If everything went according to plan, they should make McKinney by morning and then she and Sarah would board the noon train north. Once that happened, Cynthia would be able to think beyond the next day.

"Am I going to have to stay inside all the time?" Sarah asked, sounding very young. "The sky is so pretty and I like the horses. I could ride a horse in pants, couldn't I?"

Cynthia had to blink the tears away. Her father had not allowed Sarah beyond their walled backyard. It was part of what made her so unruly, Cynthia believed. If only the girl could get out and move, she would burn off the nervous energy that came with being locked in a nursery all day long.

She had a vision of Sarah taking long walks, maybe with a dog to keep her company—and keep her safe. How much would Sarah love that? She could be a part of the world around her, not separate from it.

But there was a problem with this vision. How was Cynthia going to manage Sarah in a place like Kansas City? There was too much risk of someone seeing a pretty girl and taking advantage of Sarah's friendliness. It'd be better if they could find a place with some land so Sarah would have room to roam while still being safe.

"You could. But not at night, okay? We'll save that for the daytime," Cynthia said firmly. Just because Sarah wasn't right mentally didn't mean she had to be treated like an infant. "You are most definitely not going to have to stay inside. You have to stay close to me," she added, mindful of the realities of the situation. "But we're going to do all sorts of fun things together."

Sarah was silent, running her fingers against Cynthia's stomach—a good sign. The tantrum had been averted. Cynthia began to doze again as the wagon shifted back and forth in a smooth pattern.

Her thoughts went right back to the Jeweled Ladies. Until the very last moment, Cam Douglas had been perfect. She had come awake to his lips brushing her forehead in a tender kiss as he whispered, "Be strong, my darlin' girl."

She'd wanted to pull him into her arms and hold onto him for just a little bit longer, but she hadn't dared. She had no claim on him and lingering never did anyone any good.

Her thoughts drifted over the scandalous evening. His easy smile, his hard body. The way he'd gripped his cock to show her how to hold it. The way he'd kissed her cunny after teaching her all the words for that secret place. The shattering pleasure he'd made her feel, so completely life-changing that she'd already forgotten about the pain.

The way he made her promise to always get what she needed from a man in bed and out of it.

She wondered—if she had told him who she really was and how desperate her circumstances were, what would he have done? He would have tried to protect her, of that she felt sure. But how? She wasn't about to marry a stranger. And there was still Sarah to consider.

No, the evening was just a moment in time, one that she would always look back on with fondness.

"Miss? Miss! Wake up!"

"What?" Cynthia startled, trying to sit up as Sarah mumbled in her sleep. "What's going on?" She could hear it—the pounding of hoof beats on hard earth. Someone was riding hard and fast in their direction.

"You stay down and keep her quiet," Mr. Shane said and Cynthia saw the dull barrel of a pistol in the dim light of the lantern. He snapped the reins and suddenly, the horses were moving much faster.

A gunshot broke the air, but she didn't hear splintering wood or Mr. Shane cry out. Whoever was behind them was a terrible shot.

"Stop or I'll shoot for real this time," the man shouted. Cynthia could barely make out the words over the sounds of Mr. Shane firing back.

"Sissy?" Sarah whimpered, clutching at Cynthia's waist.

"Stay down," she said, shoving her sister flat and laying the carpetbags on top of her. "Be quiet, sweetie. No matter what, be quiet."

Her mind raced. They'd caught her—that much was obvious. But maybe whoever had been sent to take her back didn't know about Sarah. If she could only keep the girl hidden, maybe Mr. Shane could get her away—

"I *will* shoot you," the man called out. He was close enough now that Cynthia could see the light from the lantern falling upon the horse. The rider was a big man, his hat pulled low over his brow and a bandanna over his nose. "I don't want to, but I will. Stop, Goddamnit!"

In response, Mr. Shane turned and shot over his shoulder. They were all going hell for leather and the man ducked. But somehow, Cynthia knew that if he shot at Mr. Shane, he wouldn't miss.

Sarah moaned loudly, but Cynthia ignored her. There was something about the man as he rode beside of them. It wasn't possible that he seemed familiar, was it? It wasn't like she consorted with robbers and criminals on a regular basis.

Then she caught sight of his eyes and startled. Before she could make sense of the fact that he'd come after her, he pulled down the bandanna. "Cynthia? Stop!"

"Cam?"

"Please," he begged and it was then she saw the red running down his arm, the hole in his coat.

It felt like time slowed down. She looked from him to where Mr. Shane sat on the bench of the wagon. He'd turned around and was balancing his pistol on his other arm. He had Cam dead to rights.

Cynthia moved without thinking. Her hands closed around the tin pail the Jewels' cook had packed some food in and she swung at Mr. Shane. She'd been aiming for the pistol, but at that exact moment the wagon bounced in a rut and she smacked him upside the head.

The gun went off and Sarah screamed as Mr. Shane slumped forward.

"Oh, God—oh, *God*," Sarah screamed.

Whether it was the screaming or the gunshots, the horses panicked. The reins looped around Mr. Shane's hand and his limp body lurched forward, almost toppling him out of the seat—and dragging him toward the horses' hooves.

Oh, no. She grabbed at the collar of his shirt, hanging on for dear life. He was a good man, one charged with protecting her and her sister. She couldn't let him be trampled to death.

She pulled with all her might, panic giving her strength.

"Come on," she muttered, clawing at his wrist, trying to loosen the reins. But Mr. Shane was dead weight at this point and he was too heavy for her. She almost fell over the bench but managed to get her feet locked and her hand on the reins. Using all her weight, she leaned back, pulling on the reins and Mr. Shane's arm at the same time.

The horses stopped so suddenly she toppled over the bench and sprawled across Mr. Shane's lap. Sarah screamed again and Cynthia had a heart-wrenching moment when the horses lurched forward and she thought they were going to pull her down with Mr. Shane.

"Easy," came Cam's voice. He grabbed her by the arm and yanked her back.

She sat hard on her bottom, wincing as she did so. "What are you doing here?" As he settled the horses, she saw the look of agony on his face. "What happened? Who shot you?"

He looked back the way he'd come. "I'll explain everything," he promised. "But there are some men coming after me. Don't tell them which way I went." He handed her the reins and made as if he were going to ride off into the darkness.

"But you're wounded!" she cried, which was the wrong thing to do because then Sarah began to cry from underneath all the things Cynthia had piled on top of her.

"It happens," Cam said, as if a gunshot wound to the shoulder was no big deal. "Are you hiding another person in there or do you have a dog?"

"I'm not a dog!" Sarah yelled, popping up and throwing the carpetbags off her. "I'm a girl! I mean, a boy," she said belatedly, which Cynthia took as a good sign that she remembered she was supposed to be in disguise, even if it had come a little late.

"Right," Cam said slowly. He looked back down the road again and this time, Cynthia could hear it— more hoof beats.

"Are they after you or me?" she demanded even

as she hauled Mr. Shane back so he wasn't in danger of falling off the bench.

"Me." He tried to help her but even in the dim light of the lantern she could see the blood drain from his face.

One thing was abundantly clear—she couldn't let him ride off into the dark. If the posse didn't kill him, the bullet wound might. "Get in the back," she said, "and let me do the talking."

She had no idea what was about to happen, but she wasn't going to let Cam get shot again. He tried to swing from his horse straight into the back of the wagon, but he grunted and fell, which made him shout in agony.

Sarah scooted to one side, looking like she was about to scream.

"Sarah. Sarah!" Cynthia demanded, grabbing her sister's hand. "You need to be quiet. You understand me? No sounds. This is Mr. Douglas. He's a friend of mine. He's not going to hurt us. You understand?"

Sarah blinked.

"Do you understand, *Sam*?" Cynthia said again with more force.

Sarah's eyes focused. "I'm not a baby, Sissy," she grumbled, but she sat up straighter and for a moment, Cynthia had a glimpse of the girl she could have been in a different life.

"That's my girl." She quickly took Cam's hat and set it on top of Sarah's head. "Keep that on," she said. Then she untied Cam's bandanna and tied it like a kerchief over her hair. "Is it possible to get your coat off?" she asked, rolling him so he lay on his back in the middle of the pallet.

"You're going to be the death of me, aren't you,"

he said, his voice low and weak. But he sat up as he said it. "Cut it off if you have to."

"No time." Without any finesse at all, she yanked the jacket from his arms. He sucked in a pained breath but didn't yell. Now she could hear the shouts of the men bearing down on them.

"Do I want to know?" she asked, keeping her voice low. Up on the bench, Mr. Shane groaned. "Mr. Shane, please stay quiet."

When she looked back at Cam, his face was drawn and pale. But for all that, he looked up at her as if she were an angel. She balled up the ruined coat and stuck it beneath his head. When she sat back, he grabbed her hand and kissed her palm. "I wanted to hold you again, but not like this." Then his eyes rolled back in his head and he went limp.

Stupid tears pricked her eyes. But before she could reply, the posse was upon them. "You there! Show yourselves!"

Cynthia was not a trained actress. She had never gotten up on stage or stood in front of a crowd and assumed a role written for specific part.

But she had spent the vast majority of her life pretending to be the perfect little china doll her father wanted, pretending she had no more cares in the world than when her next dress would be finished. Pretending she didn't have a sister with a heart or dreams of her own.

She let all that frustration, all that worry about Cam's shoulder, bubble up and before she knew it, she was sobbing. Sobbing for a different life that she'd never get to have.

"Oh, thank goodness!" she cried, launching herself to her feet and grabbing for the lantern at the side of the wagon. "We were just beset by a robber! He shot my husband and I'm afraid he shot our driver! He came out of nowhere," she wailed, hoping that enough of her hair was hidden beneath the bandanna. She almost wished she'd kept that terrible wig.

Thank God, she didn't recognize the face that loomed out of the dark. "This is your husband?" the man demanded.

"He is. Stuart Cooper. And I'm Betty Cooper, and this is my brother Sam," she said, hoping that Sarah remembered she was supposed to be quiet. "And Roy Harper—we hired him to drive us to McKinney."

She couldn't tell how many other men were out there, although it sounded like there were at least three others. "What are you and your husband doing out in the middle of nowhere at this time of night, ma'am?" Condescension dripped from his voice.

She dropped her gaze and let the shame burn through her cheeks. "We couldn't pay the rent," she said weakly. "We had to leave in a hurry."

The man snorted. Clearly, he wasn't buying this tale. If she couldn't convince them, she didn't want to think about what they would do to Cam—or her. "He came out of nowhere," she said, desperate to turn the conversation away from her supposed marriage. "My husband tried to get off a shot, but we couldn't even see him in the dark. He was riding a dark horse and wearing a black coat." Both of which were true.

Wait, where *was* Cam's horse? She looked around and saw that Sarah was standing in the wagon, the reins of the animal in her hands. She petted the poor creature's head and murmured to it.

Cynthia sent a silent prayer Sarah wouldn't get it

into her head to try riding the horse right now. Hopefully the posse wouldn't notice how lathered up the animal was.

She went on, "He had a bandanna over his face and he tried to murder my husband." She dropped her face into her hands and began to cry harder.

"Betty," Cam said in a rough voice. She startled. Was he awake? "For God's sake, woman. It's just a flesh wound." He tried to push himself up into a sitting position, grimacing. "My wife is right."

"Where are you people coming from?" the man on horseback asked, sounding slightly less doubtful.

"Grapevine Springs," Cam said as Cynthia helped push him into an upright position. "A ranch owner by the name of Evans hired me on, but he didn't pay the wages we agreed on. Said he'd have us arrested if we didn't pay the rent he was charging us for a shack."

Cynthia was stunned when the man on horseback leaned over and spit. "Yeah, Evans is a bastard. Where you headed?"

It certainly helped that Cam knew the area better than she did. "Dallas, for starters. After that... " He tried to shrug but groaned. "I didn't get a good look at the bastard. I got a shot off, but I'm not much of a gunfighter," he said with a rueful smile. He pointed north, wincing. "He went that way. I hope you catch him. He shot me, injured our driver and scared my wife, and I'm not going to stand for that."

"You will most certainly sit," Cynthia snapped, trying to sound like a worried wife. "I won't lose you, Stuart."

Cam turned to look at her and she could see the worry in his eyes, plain as day.

The man on horseback chuckled. "Try to avoid gunfights in the future and consider traveling during daylight hours when it's safer." He wheeled his horse around and called out to the rest of his posse and they were off, thundering north.

Cam collapsed back, his eyes closed, his brow furrowed with pain. "Thank you," he murmured.

Cynthia smoothed his hair away from his forehead. "You're hurt. I wouldn't give you up. Not to them."

Sarah crouched next to Cynthia and peered down at the strange man who was bleeding all over everything. "Are you going to die?" she asked with her usual bluntness.

Cynthia stared at her sister. She would've expected the girl to dissolve into hysterics because Sarah did not like blood. Her monthly courses were always a time of trauma for the entire household. That, paired with the fact that her carefully ordered world had been completely upended over the last twenty-four hours, would've usually pitched Sarah into a tantrum that would've taken Cynthia and three or four maids to calm her.

But now? Here, under the wide-open sky in the shadow of darkness, with a horse's reins in her hands, Sarah was someone else. Someone braver and more capable.

Cam lay on the floor of the wagon, bleeding. Cynthia had hit Mr. Shane upside the head. She had no idea how far they were from McKinney, but when Cam smiled at Sarah and said, "I bet you like fairytales," Cynthia knew that somehow, everything was all going to be all right.

Sarah smiled that warm, welcoming smile that Cynthia didn't see very often. "Have you heard about Robin Hood?" the girl asked somberly, because fairytales were very serious to Sarah.

That's when Mr. Shane's head popped over the back of the bench, a pistol in his hand as he asked, "So, do I need to shoot him or not?"

Chapter Eleven

No!" Cynthia cried in a panic. "Please don't. I know him. He's a friend."

Friends. Sure. That's what they were calling it these days, when he spent an evening debauching a virgin and robbing a bank, only to have said former virgin come to his rescue.

Cam managed to tilt his head back, his vision swimming. A dark face peered over the bench seat of the wagon and a pistol pointed straight at him. "I'd prefer not to be shot. Again. Hope I missed you," he mumbled, his mouth feeling dry.

He began to float in the darkness and he hated that feeling. He could hear Cynthia making noises, sounding apologetic.

If he were going to die, this wasn't a bad way to go. Cynthia sat next to him, holding his hand like an angel who had appeared out of the night to save him from the posse.

Something poked him in the leg. "Sissy says you're nice but I don't know. Are you?" the girl dressed up like a boy asked.

"Sarah, let him alone. He's hurt," Cynthia said in a patient voice.

Sarah. So much more about the situation made

sense now. He wanted to protect Cynthia, but it was clear Cynthia was protecting Sarah. Was she why Cynthia had gone through with the auction? Was this girl the reason she needed the money?

It had to be part of it—but that didn't explain why Cynthia had wanted to be ruined quite so much. And he was in too much pain to figure that one out.

"I'm so sorry I hit you, Mr. Shane. I didn't want you to shoot him. I was trying to hit your gun... " Cynthia said.

The black man snorted. "Did I get him or was he already like that?"

"Not you," Cam got out through gritted teeth.

The wagon shifted and he had to fight back a scream. Then strong hands were on him. "Sorry about your shirt," the man said and then a knife sliced the fabric away from his shoulder and Cam might have blacked out again.

He just wanted to sink down into the darkness, where the pain in his shoulder was a memory instead of a living thing determined to claw him to pieces. But suddenly his shoulder was burning and he was screaming and trying to move but someone held him down. Or sat on him.

"Shh, shh," a soft voice said, cool hands on his face. "He's getting the bullet out."

A girl began to cry, but it didn't sound like Cynthia. She wouldn't cry over him, would she?

"'S okay," he tried to say when the burning stopped for a second. "Don't cry."

"Blood is bad," the girl sobbed.

"Sarah, honey, why don't you look at the sky and tell Mr. Douglas a story, okay? He'd like to hear about

Maid Marian," Cynthia said in the same soft voice. "And be sure to keep petting that horse. I think he likes you."

He could hear the pleading tone in her voice. "Thunder likes pretty girls," Cam got out.

"This is gonna hurt," the man said and then liquid fire licked through Cam, burning him to ashes, leaving him hollow. He was pain and fire and nothing more.

Then it all eased back and he gasped for breath. From somewhere that sounded very far away, he heard a singsong voice saying, "And she lived in a castle where mean old King John kept her locked away... "

"Hatfield," Cam said, pushing back against the agony. "The boy." Where was the boy?

He must've tried to sit up, because strong hands were pushing him back down. "You were alone," Cynthia said. Something soft and warm pressed against his forehead.

He'd lost Hatfield. Goddamnit, he never should've taken this bank job. Now he was wounded and Hatfield might be dead and Cam couldn't even remember if they'd gotten the money. If Hatfield died for nothing, Cam didn't know how he'd live with himself.

Of course, he might not live at all. The burning bled into pressure that felt like his arm was being ripped off his body and Cam gave up the fight to stay awake. He let himself sink into the warmth of Cynthia against his chest, her hands on his face, her scent filling his nose.

He'd wanted to hold her one more time.

It was a hell of a last request.

"Michael, row the boat ashore, halleluiah."

Cam tried to open his eyes but they didn't work. It was dark and a warm weight pressed against his side and voices sang an old spiritual.

Was he dead? Were those angels singing? If so, had he actually made it into heaven?

"Then you'll hear the trumpet blow, hallel-u-u-u-uiah." The voices' singing split apart, the higher one warbling off key.

The deeper voice rumbled with an easy laugh. "Don't get too fancy there."

"Can we sing it again?" the higher voice said. Cam thought he heard clapping.

They launched into the song again. Cam almost smiled.

The warm weight against his side stirred. "Cam?" a soft voice breathed against his ear. "Are you awake?"

Cynthia. Maybe he really had died and gone to a heaven where angels didn't always sing in key, because Cynthia was with him. "Depends. Am I dead?"

She sighed against him, and then something warm pressed against his neck. A kiss. He jolted and then moaned as his shoulder began to throb. "I don't think a dead man would be able to feel that." He could feel the curve of her mouth against his skin.

If his shoulder weren't trying to kill him and if there weren't people sitting right behind his head, repeating the same two verses of a song over and over again, he'd roll into Cynthia and lose himself in that smile, in her kisses.

But he was wounded. He'd... he'd been shot. The bank.

Shit. The job.

"Where are we?"

"*Hallel-u-u-u-uiah-h-h-h,*" they sang.

Sarah, the sister dressed as a brother. He remembered now. And a black man who'd tried to shoot him but then cut a bullet out of him.

He'd lost Hatfield in the gunfight.

Shit.

"My horse?"

"Shh," Cynthia whispered, her mouth right against his ear. "He's tied to the back of the wagon. Mr. Shane gave him some water. He's okay."

"Saddlebags?" he said as quietly as he could.

"They're on the horse. There's four of them. They look... heavy."

That was something, then. If he had to guess, he'd say he'd gotten almost eight thousand dollars out of the bank before the world had exploded around him and Hatfield.

Cam was not a praying sort of man. Hadn't been to church since his mother died back when he'd been fourteen. Cam knew too much of the world, of how men dressed up their sins as virtues.

But as he lay in Cynthia's arms, the spiritual echoing out into the night, he prayed hard that Hatfield had gotten away. The boy deserved better than to suffer for Cam's stupidity.

"We didn't look in the saddlebags," she whispered against his ear and belatedly he realized that she didn't want the other man to know Cam was awake. "But later? You're going to explain yourself to me, Cam Douglas." She thumped him on the chest for emphasis.

He smiled again and this time, he was able to get his eyes open. Pink light streaked across the sky, a Texas dawn letting him know he was still alive. "Where are we going?"

"McKinney. We're supposed to catch a train to Kansas City." She shifted against him and he definitely knew he wasn't dead because his cock tried to stir. "But we'll get a room and a doctor and—"

"No." His arm tightened around her shoulders. "Kansas City is good. I'll go with you."

"But you're wounded!" she hissed. "You need a doctor!"

"They'll catch us if we stay. We need to get out of Texas. Besides, they're going to be looking for a man alone and two women. A husband and wife travelling with a boy won't be noticed."

Even as he said it, his mind spun out a fantasy, one that started with him and Cynthia getting married and ended with them in bed. A proper wedding night—that's what he'd give her this time. There was so much more he could teach her—how to bend over the edge of the bed and spread her legs wide so he could watch his cock slam into her cunny until he made her scream with pleasure. How to mount up on him and ride him hard so he could pull at her nipples until her sweet heat clamped down on his cock and she milked him dry.

He could love her for a lifetime, if only she'd let him.

He slid his good arm down her waist, pulled her up to his lips. This was crazy. But really, was it any crazier than buying a virgin at auction? "Cynthia."

"Hmm?"

"Marry me."

118

Chapter Twelve

S he hadn't said yes. Of course, she hadn't said no, either.

"Yes, we need an additional ticket. If you have a private sleeping berth? And is there space for a horse in the livestock car?" Cynthia was politely making a nuisance of herself at the ticket window. The conversation would probably go faster if Cam were the one buying, but it was all he could do to stand upright and not black out.

Sarah stood next to him, her eyes round as she patted Thunder's nose. She wasn't quite right, Cam had realized somewhere around the fortieth version of "Michael Row the Boat Ashore." Childlike, he decided. She was a grown woman, or close to it, but her mind didn't seem quite matched up to her body.

No wonder Cynthia was protective of her.

"I forgot the name," he ground out through gritted teeth, "of Robin Hood's best friend."

Sarah's head whipped around and she looked at him as if he were stupid. "Little John, of course. Everyone knows that."

Despite the pain and the exhaustion, he managed to smile for her. "And they found a sword in a lake, right?"

Cynthia glanced back over her shoulder and sent him a grateful smile as Sarah launched into a full-on lecture about the differences between King Arthur and Robin Hood. The young girl knew her fairytales.

Aside from being shot and losing Hatfield, things were working out. He'd survived his escape from Brimstone and as a bonus, he was now traveling with Cynthia. Sure, that came with an additional sister, but it provided good cover.

He hadn't needed to ask Cynthia to marry him to travel together. He had anyway.

But she hadn't said yes.

At least it was just the three of them now. The man who had driven the wagon, Mr. Shane, had left them at the station. He'd refused any sort of payment, even when Cam had tried to give him Thunder. He was secretly pleased the man had said no because Lady Ruby was covering his costs. Thunder was a hell of a good horse, but Cam had been trying to do the right thing.

Cynthia turned back to them and immediately came to his good side, wrapping her arm around his waist. "They had one sleeping car left—and the good news is that it's private. Four berths, a washstand and its own door. Plus, we got the last stall for the horse. It was expensive, though."

He could hear the worry in her voice even as he leaned on her more heavily. "Doesn't matter. I have the money."

"Stay here. I'll see to the horse."

He wished he had the strength to argue, but she left him leaning against a wall. A porter came for the horse and Sarah looked upset that Thunder was being led away. But Cynthia soothed her and the girl only pouted a little. She could pass as a young man. That was good for their mad escape from Brimstone.

He was wounded and barely able to stand. Yet as he watched Cynthia square her shoulders and lift her chin, he smiled all the same. She was a rare woman, his Cynthia. Maybe he shouldn't have blurted out a marriage proposal like he had.

But if he had to do it over again... Cynthia glanced back at him and smiled. Not big, just a small curve of her lips when their eyes met.

Cam had never figured himself as the kind to settle down, but there was something about her. He'd seen it from the very first, in the middle of a dusty street and then again when he'd bought her night. He'd prayed for another night to hold her in his arms, hadn't he?

Somehow, getting shot was the answer to his prayers. Odd, that.

She walked back to him, one of the saddlebags over her shoulders, one over her sister's. "Can you walk onto the train?"

Yeah, he'd ask her again. He nodded. She got under his side, her body light and warm against his, and despite the gunshot wound, his cock tried to stir at her touch.

Somehow, they made it onto the train. They were at the front, in the nice cars the wealthy used to keep themselves separate from the rabble and the animals. They were going to be mighty out of place here.

But it didn't matter. Cynthia was by his side. He could walk to Missouri, so long as she stayed with him.

"Does the train go all the way to Kansas City?" he asked as they made their way to their berth. It felt odd, only having the saddlebags and two carpetbags. And the carpetbags weren't even his.

"Yes." The conductor showed them to their berth and Cam almost wept at the sight. Cynthia sat him on a lower bunk and helped him swing his legs over the edge and then said, "I'm going to show Sarah around. We'll be back."

"Promise," he said, even as he sank back into the bed.

She smoothed his hair away from his face, her touch warming him from the inside out. "I promise," she said and then she kissed him, right on the lips.

As he drifted off, he found himself hoping that, when he woke up, she'd say yes.

*

"He doesn't know a lot about fairytales," Sarah said as they explored the dining car.

Cynthia hid a smile behind her hand as she showed Sarah how to order from the menu. "True. But what's important is that he's willing to learn." That was a phrase that Cynthia used on an almost daily basis with her sister.

Sarah nodded wisely. "Very important. Are we going to stay with him?"

"For now." The man had asked Cynthia to marry him. She had no idea if that was a legitimate proposal or a fevered delusion. After all, he hadn't been terribly awake this morning and he had been in a great deal of pain.

Even if he had seriously proposed, she had several questions of her own. Like why he had been racing away from Brimstone with a gunshot wound to his shoulder? And what was in those saddlebags? To say nothing of who this Hatfield was and where he might be.

But for all of that—and Cynthia suspected she would not like the answers to those questions—there was still something thrilling about the proposal. He had asked her. Not her father, not anyone else. *Her.* He'd already made love to her. He thought she was strong and brave. And Sarah liked him. At this point, was there much difference between a pretend marriage and a real one?

"Sissy?" Sarah tugged on her arm and Cynthia realized she had been lost in her own thoughts.

"Yes, sweetie?"

"He's going to sleep, right? It would be rude if I opened up the blinds and watched out the window while he was sleeping, right? So," she went on in a rush, "can I sit here—right here—and watch out the window? I'll be good. I promise." Sarah clapped her hands in front of herself, looking hopeful. She still had on Cam's hat, which sat low over her ears and hid a great deal of her face.

Cynthia considered her options. If she said no and made Sarah come back to their berth, the girl might pitch a fit. And if Cynthia said yes, Sarah would be happy for at least twenty minutes. That would give Cynthia time to go back and check on Cam.

It really wasn't much of a decision. "You have to sit right here and not bother anyone. Just look out the window. And if you start to feel fussy, you have to come right back."

Sarah nodded eagerly, starting to hop. "I'll be extra good. This is so exciting!" She slid into the chair and fixed her gaze out the window with fierce dedication.

Grinning, Cynthia turned and hurried back to the sleeping berth. She did draw the blind, but only halfway. There was a pitcher in the washstand bolted to the wall and she filled up the basin and then rummaged around for one of her petticoats. She tore off a length of one and moved over to where Cam slept. Cynthia and Mr. Shane had managed to get the shirt and coat she'd bought at the general store on him after tying a bandanna over the gunshot wound.

"Cam?" She leaned over him and gently shook his uninjured shoulder. "Can you sit up? I need to look at your wound."

He blinked and then scrubbed at his face with his good hand. "Oh, thank God. I was afraid I'd dreamed you." He cupped her cheek and then slid his hand to her hair, pulling her down to him. "I don't want this to be a dream," he murmured and then she was kissing him and he was kissing her and it was all Cynthia could do to keep from falling all over him.

But apparently that was what he wanted. He pulled her onto him so she lay halfway across his chest. She had to prop herself up on her hands to make sure she wasn't adding any weight to his shoulder, but that just drove her hips into his. Instantly she could feel the hot, hard length of his cock against her. "You're wounded," she said, gasping as she broke the kiss.

"Don't care. I only care that you're here," he said, pulling her mouth down to his again. "If I'm going to die, I want to have you one last time."

"I don't want you to die." As she spoke, his hand skimmed down her back until he could grab her skirts. He began to pull, baring her legs.

"Don't deny me this," he said, his voice rough. "I need you. God, I need you. Have since I ran into you in the street."

She began to spiral, that throbbing heaviness between her legs building again. How was he doing this to her? It took so little for him to make her body needy for him. Only him.

She jerked away. "Wait."

Before he could protest, she pushed herself off the bunk and went to the door, locking it and making sure the shade was fully pulled down. Then she moved back to stand next to him. She couldn't undress—there wasn't time. But she pulled up her skirts and undid the drawstring of her drawers so they fell away. She stepped out of them and then said, "What do I do next?"

"I have never known another woman like you," he said, his eyes falling to where her legs were bare. She lifted her skirts higher, letting him glimpse the soft hair that covered her sex. "I hope you marry me."

"I haven't decided," she said honestly. If she did, then her father lost any power he had over her. No one could force her to take Vincent Brown to her bed, where she would always be unsatisfied. Cam would always take care of her. But...

"Undo my trousers," he said, his voice rough. "Then come and sit astride of me. Take me inside your sweet cunny, my darlin' girl, and let me convince you."

She shouldn't be nervous. They had done this not so very long ago. And even though she was a little sore, she could still feel that heavy weight between her legs, pushing her to undo the buttons on his trousers, and then pluck at the drawstrings of his drawers. She shoved his clothing aside and he sprang free, somehow even more magnificent than she remembered.

"Why should I marry you?" she asked as she tucked her head to fit underneath the upper sleeping berth. She straddled him so that his big cock pressed against her. "And don't just say because you're good at this," she said as he reached up with his good hand and undid the top buttons on her plain brown traveling dress.

Cynthia shifted back and forth, letting her tired muscles wake up, letting his length stroke against her sensitive pearl. He had said that when she was wet for him, it was easier. She didn't think she was ready just yet.

"Well, *we* are," he said, his hand slipping inside her bodice. He cupped her breast through the shift and stroked his thumb over her nipple. "We're very good together and we've only just begun." His hips began to move, shifting against her. His cock dragged over the folds of her sex, teasing without satisfying.

"It's not enough," she gasped, bracing one hand on the wall next to his bad shoulder and the other against the berth overhead. "What kind of man would I be marrying?" He pinched her nipple then, not hard, but more than enough to send sparks of desire racing over her skin.

"I robbed a bank," he said through gritted teeth. "You were supposed to be my alibi. But you're so much more, Cynthia."

She paused, staring down at him in shock as she tried to process the words. "You robbed a bank?"

He nodded. "Got maybe eight thousand dollars in my saddlebags. I'll buy you a house. Dresses. Whatever you want."

She swallowed, trying to make sense of this. There was only one bank in Brimstone. It was why her father controlled the town. "The First Macon County Bank?"

"Yeah. Someone hired us to do it, but they wanted it done in three weeks. I didn't trust the man, so we decided to do the job early." His hand shifted to her other breast, stroking and teasing, and without conscious thought, Cynthia's hips began to move again. He felt so good against her, so right.

"You robbed the First Macon County Bank," she said, giggles bursting out of her.

"Is that funny?" he asked, an uncertain smile on his face.

"You robbed the bank," she repeated, leaning down to kiss him. As she did, she lifted her bottom in the air and suddenly, the head of his cock was against her cunny. "You robbed my *father's* bank."

And then she impaled herself upon him.

Chapter Thirteen

Cam blinked at her in shock. She couldn't have said—he couldn't have heard—"Your father owns the bank?" But even that rational thought was obliterated from his mind by the weight of Cynthia settling on his aching cock. He groaned, the pain and pleasure all blending together until there was nothing but her body taking his in.

The train shuddered and she sank onto him even farther. She winced a little. She was probably still sore—but he could tell it didn't hurt as much. Thank God for that.

"You robbed his bank," she said as the train made a few rapid back-and-forth motions. Every time the train lurched, she sank down on him farther and farther until he was buried to the hilt. "You took his money and his daughter."

For the life of him, Cam had no idea if this was a good thing or not. But she was fucking him and smiling at him and he began to think maybe it was a good thing. A very good thing.

"Yeah," he managed to get out. "I did. And I don't want to give you back."

She lifted off him, and he groaned with the pleasure of it. "You are a bad man, aren't you?"

He heard the purr in her voice. "A little bad. I robbed stagecoaches for a while." Might as well get this all out in the open.

"Did you kill people?"

"Not if I could help it. I didn't kill your friend, did I?"

She rose off him and then settled her weight on him again, the tight glove of her cunny gripping him. If he died now, he'd go a damned happy man. "No, you didn't."

She grabbed his hand and guided it back to the inside of her dress, so that he could stroke her nipples again. He smiled then. She'd learned her lessons well, it seemed. She knew what she wanted and she wasn't afraid to ask for it.

"Sarah has to stay with me," she said, rising and falling and driving him slowly out of his mind. She had no great skill, but he hadn't expected it. Somehow, it was all the sweeter because of that. "She'll always have to stay with me, but I won't let anyone hurt her." She rested her full weight on him, pinning him to the berth. Then she leaned forward and, after a moment's hesitation, put her hand on his exposed throat. She leaned forward, putting the barest of pressure on him. "Including you."

She was ferocious, his Cynthia. "God, I could love you," he said, smiling up at her.

She pulled her hand back. "Excuse me?" The train lurched again and she seemed to remember that he was buried inside of her. Slowly, she pulled herself free of him and then slid back down.

"You are, without a doubt, the strongest, bravest woman I have ever met," he said, using his free hand to grip her hips and help her set the rhythm. He couldn't do much. All he could do was lie here and take it. Take everything she could give him and more.

She gave him a sad little smile that just about broke his heart. "I don't feel very brave, Cam. I'm scared most of the time."

That was probably the truth. She'd been terrified during the auction. He probably scared the hell out of her when he'd come upon that wagon in the darkness and then, when she'd realized that he'd been shot, that hadn't been good either.

But she hadn't run screaming at any of it. She'd trusted herself to him on more than one occasion, her chin up and her shoulders back. Even as she rode him, her hips shifting faster and faster, she had that proud set to her shoulders. He would never find another woman like her.

"Lift your skirts up," he ordered, his stones beginning to tighten. She gave him a questioning look, then did as he ordered.

It hurt too much to lift his head and watch when he slid into her, so instead he let his fingers explore for him. He stroked that soft bit of skin of her inner thigh and then up to her curls. There it was—a little pearl, the seat of all her pleasure. He pressed against it with his thumb and was rewarded with a powerful shudder that shook her entire body.

"You robbed my father's bank," she said, fisting her hand in his shirt and bearing down on his thumb and his cock.

"I did," he said, rolling his thumb back and forth across her sensitive button. "And I stole his daughter." It was hard to think because all he could do was feel the tight, wet heat of her cunny around him, the way she bore down on his hand.

She was running away from her father. She was running away from that bank. And once again, it had let her straight to his arms.

"Come for me, my darlin' girl," he said as his cock began to jerk with the force of his climax. "Be mine."

She cried out and he felt her body squeeze his cock tight. He couldn't fight the climax as it tore through him, blissfully blocking out the pain in his shoulder for one glorious, wonderful moment.

It was only when she collapsed upon his chest, both breathing hard, and his softening cock beginning to pull free of her tight embrace that he realized—no sheath. The moment that thought crossed his mind, it was followed by another—if he got her with child, she'd *have* to marry him.

Reluctantly, she pulled herself off him. "What were you going to do with my father's money?"

It took a moment for his head to stop swimming. He was suddenly exhausted and all he wanted to do was hold her against him while he slept. "I was going to retire, buy some land in the Ozark Mountains in Missouri, raise Missouri Fox Trotters."

"So you're done robbing?" A cool cloth touched his cock, cleaning him up.

"Yeah." Why would he continue a life of crime? A piece of land, his own horses—and Cynthia by his side? There could even be children. Their children. It was true that Sarah was part of the deal, but he didn't see that as a bad thing. She might need some extra patience, but...

He remembered her petting Thunder. "Did your sister like my horse?"

"Yes. She'd like to ride one someday." He felt her hands on him, pushing back the too-large coat and shirt. "Good, it's not bleeding. I'm going to go get Sarah and you are going to sleep."

"Marry me," he murmured, already slipping off into the darkness.

The door clicked shut behind her.

She still hadn't answered.

*

Dazed, Cynthia hurried back to the dining car. She hated leaving Sarah alone, especially in a strange place like a train. There was no right answer, she felt. Hopefully, the girl hadn't panicked while Cynthia had been...

Well. She'd been having sex with Cam. Stupid, *stupid*.

Cam, who'd bought her at an auction because he recognized the set of her shoulders. Cam, who'd taken great care with her for her first time. Cam, who'd given her amazing pleasure. Cam, who'd robbed her father's bank and been shot in the process.

Cam, who'd asked her to marry him and appeared to mean it.

Oh, thank God—Sarah was sitting right where Cynthia had left her. She drummed her fingers against the table at an increasingly frantic speed, but all appeared to be well for the moment.

"Sweetie? Look how good you're sitting," Cynthia said, sliding in next to her sister and wrapping her arm around her shoulder. "Did you have fun?"

Sarah was silent for a moment—a moment too

long—and Cynthia began to wonder if something had happened. "I'm sad about Doreen," she said, her voice small.

Cynthia sighed inwardly. "Honey, we couldn't bring Doreen with us. I know she misses you too, but she would be happy that you're getting to do all sorts of fun things. You're doing great on the train. Isn't this fun?" she said, hoping her voice didn't sound too forced.

Sarah shrugged. "I want to pet the horse again."

Sarah had no idea if they were allowed to go back and visit the animals while they were moving. Cam would know, though. "We can't do anything with Mr. Douglas's horse without Mr. Douglas. And right now, he's taking a nap."

Sarah whimpered, which was not a good sign.

"We have two choices," Cynthia went on, unsure which one was the best option. "We can sit here for another forty-five minutes while Mr. Douglas rests and then go see if he wants to look at the horse or we can both go back and take a nap now and pet the horse when we wake up." Frankly, Cynthia could do with a nap and heaven only knew how Sarah was not currently melting down. She'd had very little sleep last night and that was never good.

"But I want to see Thunder now," she whined, her voice getting louder.

"Sarah," Cynthia said, her voice severe. "We cannot go see the horse if you cannot be calm. Mr. Douglas will not want his horse frightened. You have to be good so you can show him he can trust you with his animal."

The argument was perfectly fine. But logic did

133

not always work with Sarah, and Cynthia braced for the worst.

Sarah scowled and blinked several times, but instead of sobbing or launching into a fit, she went back to drumming her fingertips on the tabletop. It was more of a slap with her whole hand, and several of the passengers around them kept checking to see what the noise was, but as far as Cynthia was concerned, slapping the table was vastly preferable to a full-fledged tantrum.

Several minutes passed before Sarah resumed just tapping her fingers. The landscape was a blur outside the window, and Cynthia gave herself a moment to wonder if she would ever see Texas again.

"Sarah," she began cautiously. "Do you like Mr. Douglas?"

"I like his horse," she said petulantly.

Cynthia bit her lip so she wouldn't smile. "He wants to go live in Missouri and raise horses. And he's invited us to come with him. Does that sound fun?"

It made sense on so many levels. She and Cam shared a great physical attraction—and she barely knew what she was doing. He was not the sort of man who would take advantage of Sarah just because she was available and pretty. And a farm—that would be a good place for Sarah. She would be able to roam a little without too much danger—plus she could ride horses and have a dog. The girl might be quite happy there.

Yes, the argument was perfectly fine. But did that make it the right choice? It was one thing to think about sharing a bed with Cam for the rest of her life. There was more to a marriage than that.

Sarah sucked on her lower lip, making a little whistling noise as she thought. "Do you think I could? Help with horses, that is?"

Cynthia's heart broke a little bit. Her entire life, Sarah had been told she couldn't do anything. She couldn't go outside, she couldn't have friends beyond Cynthia and the maids. According to their father, she was worthless and hopeless, but that's not what Cynthia saw. There was so much the girl could do. Even if she was never able to marry and raise her own family, Sarah had a great deal to give this world. All she needed was the chance.

"I think you might—as long as you do as Mr. Douglas tells you to when it comes to the horses. And you can always help me, too. If we decide to stay with him, I'll be in charge of the house."

Sarah stopped sucking on her lip and stared at Cynthia. "Would you be married?"

Cynthia nodded. "Mr. Douglas and I would be married, yes. But you would always stay with me. No one would keep us apart."

"What about Father?" Even as she said it, Sarah seemed to shrink into herself. "I don't think he'd like that."

Cynthia gritted her teeth and did something she very rarely had to do—she lied to her sister. "Actually, Father gave his blessing. He gave Mr. Douglas some money as a wedding present for us. Because he wants us to be happy."

It was such a bold lie that not even Sarah believed it. She scrunched up her face, looking doubtful. Gerald Hobbs was not known for wishing anyone happiness, especially not his simple daughter. Cynthia kept her smile wide and bright. And that seemed to be enough for Sarah.

"Will he be nice to me? Not like that other man was."

Cynthia's heart broke a little more. She didn't know exactly what Vincent Brown had done to her sister, although she feared the worst. Had he gone up to the nursery and assaulted Sarah? Or had Father just paraded the girl before him, like livestock at auction? Cynthia didn't know and she hated not knowing. Her job was to protect Sarah and she felt like she had failed.

But wasn't that just another reason why Cynthia should take Cam Douglas up on his offer? If she were married to Cam, safely tucked away in Missouri, her father and Vincent would have no claim on her or Sarah. None.

"I think so," Cynthia said honestly. After all, Cam said that he would never hurt a woman. "He likes fairytales and he's good with horses." And Cynthia did like him, quite a bit.

Sarah nodded thoughtfully. Fairytales and horses were serious matter to her. "Maybe it would be okay," she said. "Maybe we would be okay."

Cynthia laced her fingers with Sarah's. "We *will* be okay."

They sat in silence for a while longer, watching the landscape blur past them. Already, it was changing as they steamed north, away from Brimstone and the only life they'd known.

She could marry Cam. She could keep his house and he could keep her satisfied and her sister safe. She could love him. And there could be children.

He would have to agree to some rules, though. No bank robbing, no stagecoach holdups. He was going to have to be an honest man if he was going to be hers. And a faithful one. She couldn't do anything about the life he'd lived before, but if he intended to marry her and carry on as he had before, she wouldn't stand for it.

Unexpectedly, she laughed out loud. She was seriously considering this. It was crazy and impulsive and perhaps not the most intelligent of moves. But then again, was this any different than throwing herself upon the mercies of the Jeweled Ladies? If anything, this was a much more rational decision.

Sarah began to get antsy and Cynthia figured enough time had passed. So they went back to their berth to ask Cam if they could pet a horse.

Chapter Fourteen

S he always been like this?"

"No," Cynthia said slowly. "I mean, yes—but no."

That didn't make a hell of a lot of sense. But most of Cam's energy was focused on standing. The rest was watching Sarah—who was still dressed as Sam—sitting on the floor of the livestock car of the train, cradling Thunder's head in her lap and crooning to him softly. Thunder, shameless hussy that he was, nuzzled his nose against Sarah's fingers, demanding even more stroking.

Which meant Cam did not have a lot of leftover brainpower to puzzle through Cynthia's quiet statement. Luckily, she explained herself anyway. "I would've thought that, by now, she would've thrown a fit. She hasn't slept. We're far outside of her normal routine. We've been in the company of strangers—no offense," she added, sounding embarrassed.

Cam looked down to see her cheeks pinking prettily. "None taken."

"I always knew there was more to her," Cynthia went on quietly. "Our father had *so* many rules. Sarah wasn't allowed to have friends. She was not allowed out of the house except into our walled backyard. He didn't even really want her out of the nursery. All she had was me and our maid. I always thought... " Her voice broke and she paused.

Cam gave her the space to get herself together.

"I always thought that if she could just get out of the house, move around a little more, have a pet or a few friends—friends who would not judge her for who she is and would not take advantage of her—that she would be so much happier. That *we* would be so much happier."

He had his arm around her shoulders, since she was more or less holding him up at this point. But he gave her a little squeeze. "Smart and beautiful. I don't know how I got this lucky."

Something Lady Ruby had said to him weeks ago came back to Cam. One never did know—this was America, after all. Circumstances could change in a heartbeat.

"So she's why you're running?" he asked, pointing with his chin to Sarah, who was now braiding Thunder's forelock.

"Yes. And no."

Cam chuckled. "You're going to keep me on my toes, aren't you?" Point of fact, she had not yet agreed to marry him, but Cam had a feeling she would.

It would be best if they could get married now. Immediately. Barring that, at the very next town that had a preacher. If she had a ring and he had a piece of paper that said they were husband and wife, they'd all be much safer. But pushing her wasn't the answer. He wanted to be on her side, not in opposition to her.

Besides, he wasn't able to do much of anything at this point. He'd slept hard after she had slipped out of their berth, the gunshot wound and the good sex leaving him drained. Even now, all he wanted to do was go back and curl his body around hers and sleep some more. It would be a few days before he was good for much of anything—including marrying.

"My father wanted to give me to a man named Vincent Brown. He's the vice president of the bank you robbed," she said softly, as if she were afraid her sister might hear the name over the sounds of her singing to a horse.

Vincent Brown? Cam and Hatfield had been in the bank's safe, shoving bundles of money into the saddlebags when the security guard—whom they had knocked out and gagged—had suddenly called out, "Mr. Brown—robbers!"

Which was an interesting thing to think about. Why was the vice president of the bank there at three-thirty in the morning?

Cam wished his mind were a little clearer. He needed more sleep and less pain before he could puzzle through that. But he had a feeling Vincent Brown was involved with the plan to rob the bank. It was possible. It might even be the truth.

He also remembered the first time he'd seen Cynthia, when she'd squared her shoulders and strode into the bank as if she were ready to do battle. "Let me guess, you weren't interested in the marriage?"

She shook her head. "Nor was I interested in letting him have my sister. But that was the deal. He would take both of us off my father's hands."

Cam grimaced, a bad taste in his mouth. "So that's why there was the auction."

"I needed the money to get her away. To get both of us away." She sighed into him, and he enjoyed the feeling of her body pressed against his. "Why did you rob the bank? I mean, besides someone hiring you to do it."

He didn't remember telling her that, but he must have. "I'm tired of robbing stagecoaches, tired of being shot at. Being shot," he corrected. "I wanted… "

Her arms were around his waist and her head was against his shoulder. She was taking a fair amount of his weight as they stood there and watched Sarah pet Thunder.

"I haven't been able to stop thinking about you since I ran into you on the street that day," he admitted. "But I knew you were a proper lady, someone who would need more than what a stagecoach robber could give you. It was foolish, but I thought if I had the money from the bank, I could set myself up as a gentleman farmer. It would still be a rough life, but it might be good enough for someone like you. That's why we pulled the job."

She gasped and went very still against him. Not even the rocking of the train seemed to move her.

They rode in silence, except for the sound of Sarah singing. Thunder exhaled heavily, clearly in heaven with all the attention he was getting. Cam focused on breathing evenly. His shoulder hurt and his legs felt like lead, but he didn't think the wound was infected. He'd been shot. That was all. It was enough.

He looked down at his feet, making sure the saddlebags were still there. That was his future. Everything he needed was here. The money, Cynthia, the horse—it was all here. Even Sarah was all right, because she had a natural way with Thunder. She'd be good with horses.

"It won't always be like this," Cynthia said, her voice barely audible above the clacking of the rails. "She's going to have bad days and throw fits. She's going to be difficult at times."

Was she trying to talk him out of marriage? If so, she was doing a lousy job of it. "Isn't that true for us all? I mess up. I mess up all the time. I make mistakes—like robbing a bank and losing my partner."

Once they were safe, he'd find out what he could about Hatfield. He prayed Lady Ruby would be able to come up with something. Lord, but he hoped the boy was safe.

"I'm not a knight in shining armor, Cynthia—but I think I'm a good man and I'd be a better one for you. I'm giving up the outlaw life. No more robbing, no more shooting. And," he added, because he knew it was on her mind, "no more whoring. I want to settle down. Raise some horses and some babies. With you. Only with you."

She looked up at him and he managed to look down without losing his balance. Her eyes shone brightly and she had the most beautiful smile on her face. "I think you'd make a fine husband, Cam Douglas."

He wanted to touch her, but he was still having trouble moving his arm and his good one was wrapped around her shoulders. So instead, he leaned down and pressed a kiss to her forehead. "And I think you'd make a fine wife, Cynthia. A fine family," he added, nodding in Sarah's direction. "Will you marry me and let me take care of you in bed and out of it?"

"Yes," she said, her voice breaking. "I don't need a fancy gentleman and I don't need to be pampered and protected. I just need you."

And then he was kissing her and she was kissing him and he had just slid his hand along her ribs, up toward her sweet breast, when Sarah piped up from the floor, "Hey, what are you two doing? That's disgusting."

Cam laughed as Cynthia scolded, "Well, I'm going to marry him, so you might just see us kiss every now and then."

Sarah thought this over. Then she clamored to her feet and came to stand right in front of Cam, a dangerous look on her face. "You better treat my sister real nice," she said, waggling a finger inches from his nose. "She's my favorite person and I don't want to see her sad anymore."

"I'll make a deal with you," Cam said, unable to keep the smile off his face at this show of defiance. "I'll make sure she's happy for the rest of her life and you can help me raise horses. Sound good?"

He wasn't sure what he expected, but Sarah spun on her heels and all but flung herself at Thunder, who had sat up enough to take interest in the surroundings. "Did you hear? You and I are going to be *friends*," she said, hugging the horse around his neck.

Cam swore to God that the horse winked at him.

He looked down at the woman he was going to spend the rest of his life with. Tears shone in her eyes, but they were tears of happiness. "That," she said, cupping his face with her hand, "is a deal."

Then they sealed it with a kiss.

Epilogue

There's my darlin' girl," Cam whispered in Cynthia's ear as his hands came around her waist.

Cynthia squeaked and almost dropped the shirt she was hanging on the clothesline. "Cam! What are you—"

"Sarah's walking the new colt," he murmured as one hand stroked over her gently rounded stomach and then moved lower, pressing between her legs.

"But Mellie… " The girl who served as both cook and maid was a distant cousin of Cam's. Not only was she a much better cook than Cynthia would ever be, she never tired of singing the same songs endlessly with Sarah. The downside of that was that Mellie was always underfoot.

"I sent her to town for the mail." His other hand moved up and cupped her breast, making her nipples tighten. "So I have you all to myself for at least twenty minutes."

"But you—oh, Cam!" she gasped as he scraped his whiskers over the sensitive skin of her neck. She had the feeling she'd been about to ask a question, but he'd driven it clean from her mind. He was very good at that. Among other things. "Twenty minutes, you say?"

He growled in response and swept her legs out from under her. "Be careful!" She squeaked again. "The baby!" Of course, she was barely showing, probably no more than three or four months along. But still—he couldn't just toss her around!

"Have I told you recently how beautiful you are?" he asked, kicking open the kitchen door and then slamming it shut behind him. He covered the distance between the kitchen and their bedroom on the other side of the parlor in their neat two-story house in seconds.

She giggled, running the palms of her hands over his beard. She had grown to like it. "Just this morning, when you woke me up with a kiss."

"Wasn't enough. I need you more. Right now." He kicked the bedroom door shut behind him and laid her out on the bed. Then he was flipping up her skirts and kneeling between her legs, jerking her hips to the edge of the bed. "God, I love that you don't wear drawers," he murmured, his rough beard scraping over the tender flesh of her inner thighs.

Then his mouth was against her, his tongue stroking over her cunny and his thumb searching for her pearl.

Cynthia surrendered to his mouth, his touch. She burrowed her fingers into his hair and held on tight. In the five months that they had been married, Cam had proven over and over that he would always put her first, would always take care of her.

She loved these quick, stolen moments when he would seduce her hard and fast and leave her breathlessly happy. She loved the long nights in bed with him, the feel of his arms around her waist, the steady beating of his heart.

She loved walking out to the paddock in the afternoon and watching him work with Sarah and the horses he'd bought with the money he'd stolen from her father—their wedding gift, they'd taken to calling it. She loved sitting down to dinner with Sarah and Cam and Mellie at the end of the day and listening to Sarah excitedly relate every moment of her day as Cam stroked Cynthia's calf with his foot.

She loved that she was carrying his child. She was his—heart, body and soul. But what truly made her happy was that he was hers, too.

Pleasure began to spiral out from where he worked her body. He slid a finger inside her and her hips bucked in response. He hummed high in the back of his throat, sending another wave of need washing over her. "Cam," she said, tugging on his hair. She wanted him over her, inside of her. "*Please.*"

Twenty minutes wasn't long enough. A lifetime wasn't long enough.

He put his teeth to her pearl and she moaned, falling back on the bed. God, she loved this man. He was an outlaw and a gentleman, a robber and a rancher. He was wicked and he was also the best man she had ever known.

As her crisis began to crest, she was so, so thankful at the strange set of circumstances that had brought them together.

She broke under his skilled touch, gasping for air as he softened his kisses. Then he pulled back and, after undoing the buttons on his trousers, fit himself against her. "God, Cynthia," he said, his voice tight with desire. "I would die without you."

"Well, it's a good thing—oh, Cam!" she gasped

as he sank into her, filling her in one long stroke. "That I'm not going anywhere," she finished as her body quivered around his hot and hard length.

He tucked her knees under his arms and squeezed her breasts through the layers of her clothing. She scrabbled for something to hold, finally getting a grip on his forearms, feeling the muscles tense and tighten with each thrust.

She surrendered to him, to her body's needs. He began to pound into her harder, faster and then, just like he always did when he was getting close, he slipped his hand between her legs, finding her little pearl and rubbing it. "My… beautiful wife," he ground out through gritted teeth.

A second crisis broke over her, stealing her breath and leaving her wrung out with pleasure. It only encouraged Cam to go faster and, moments later, he threw back his head, the cords on his neck straining as he found his release deep inside of her.

He all but collapsed onto her, just managing to prop himself up so he didn't crush her belly. But that was just who he was—the man who always took care *with* her and *of* her. He was her husband and she wouldn't have anyone else.

Certainly not Vincent Brown, that toad.

Cam kissed the top of her breasts as he pulled free. "Why are you smiling?"

"I was just thinking," she said, sighing deeply has he got a cloth from the washstand and attended to her. "I may be the luckiest woman alive."

He chuckled. "You're not sure? Then I'll have to try harder, my darlin' wife. Next time—"

But before he could detail exactly how he was

going to try harder, the door to the kitchen banged open with such force it could mean only one person was inside—Sarah. Slamming doors was a thing they were all learning to live with, but Cynthia was happy Sarah could come and go as she pleased. No longer did she have to be kept locked in a nursery. "Cam?"

Cam and Cynthia's sighed in unison and then shared a smile. Their twenty minutes were up.

"Coming!" He helped her to her feet and did up his buttons while she shook her skirts down. Together they walked back to the kitchen, hand in hand. "What is it, little sister?" Cam asked and then pulled up short.

Cynthia also stumbled to a stop because behind Sarah, there was a large man and tiny woman and oddly, Cynthia recognized the man. Wasn't he the big, silent man who had guarded the stage the night she'd auctioned her virginity off at the Jeweled Ladies? He'd then sat outside her door to make sure Cam treated her well.

That didn't make any sense. But it couldn't be anyone else. "Mr. Steel?"

He nodded, but he didn't say anything.

"She said she knew Cam," Sarah said, jerking her thumb at Mr. Steel's companion. "I did what I was supposed to and brought them right here. They didn't touch any of the horses or anything." Pleased with remembering all the rules, she added, "Can Wags and I have a cookie?" Wags, Sarah's loyal hound dog—another gift from Cam—sat and perked up his ears, looking hopeful at the mention of one of his favorite words.

Cynthia nodded. "Two cookies—but you have to eat them outside."

Sarah happily moved to the cookie jar, leaving Cynthia with a clear view of her guests. She had never seen the woman standing by Mr. Steel's side before. She was delicate, with an almost elfin face. Her gown was a sumptuous deep blue silk, so fine that Cynthia was struck by an uncommon jealousy. Cam had purchased her several lovely dresses—and matching hats—but in this corner of Missouri, it was hard to get fashion that delectable.

But for all that, the woman didn't look like a Jewel. The dress was too modest, her posture too demure. There was nothing scandalous about this woman at all and besides, Cynthia didn't recognize her in the least.

"Welcome," she said, more than a little confused. Why would the man who was the bodyguard of the Jeweled Ladies have travelled here to the Douglas horse farm in Missouri in the company of a woman who wore the finest of finery? "And who is your companion?"

The woman looked oddly uncomfortable, as if her skin were too tight. Or perhaps the dress was. But she wasn't looking at Cynthia. Instead, her gaze was locked on Cam.

Before Cynthia could begin to panic that this was one of Cam's old *acquaintances* come back to haunt them, Cam stumbled forward, his jaw dropped in what looked like... horror? "Hatfield? Is that *you*? In a dress?"

Cynthia blinked. Hatfield—that'd been the name of his partner, the one he had been forced to leave behind at the bank robbery. It was Cam's one big regret, that he hadn't been able to save his friend.

149

Cynthia stared at the girl again, but she saw no sign that the person in the dress was actually a boy. Her features were too fine, her bosom too well highlighted by the stylish cut of that fabulous dress.

Her guests looked at each other. Mr. Steel gave an encouraging nod and then the girl turned to Cam. She cleared her throat and, in a voice that was light and almost airy, said, "Actually, my name is Hattie."

About the Author

Thanks so much for reading this *Jeweled Ladies* story! Leaving an honest review or telling a friend what you thought is the best way to show the love for your friendly local author!

Who is Maggie Chase? Writer, reader, crafter—I've told a lot of different stories a lot of different ways as Sarah M. Anderson, but the Jeweled Ladies series marks my first foray into historical erotica. I passionately believe that every single person deserves their own happily-ever-after and my stories reflect that hope on the page.

Readers can find out more about Maggie any of the following ways:

Sign up for her newsletter:
http://bit.ly/maggiechasenews

Visit her website:
http://www.maggiechase.com

Check out her Tumblr:
http://themaggiechase.tumblr.com/

Follow on Twitter:
http://twitter.com/TheMaggieChase

Leave a review on Goodreads:
http://www.goodreads.com/maggie_chase

Get Amazon pre-order information:
www.amazon.com/author/maggiechase

Other Books by Maggie Chase

The Jeweled Ladies: The Mistress Series

His Topaz
Their Emerald
Her Ebony
His Sapphire
His Crown Jewel

The Jeweled Ladies: The Rogues Series

His Diamond
His Amethyst

Now Available from Maggie Chase

Civil War veteran Matthew Hawkins needs one night to feel whole again. But when he's paired up with Miss Topaz Gold, he isn't ready for how the vulnerable young woman will claim his heart. Can he convince her to marry him—or will she stay at the Jeweled Ladies?

Read on for an excerpt of
HIS TOPAZ
The first Jeweled Ladies story

He shouldn't have come to this place. But a man had needs and Matthew Hawkins was being crushed by the loneliness of his life. Besides, the girl the madam of this brothel was leading him toward was pretty.

No, she wasn't. She was absolutely *stunning*, a vision of gold. The light of the gas lamps made her curly blonde hair glow as if she were an angel and her pale skin was a creamy ivory. She was almost too beautiful—far too fine a lady for the likes of him.

But the madam of this brothel had promised that she had the right woman for him, and Matthew needed a woman. Just for one night. Then he could go back to the ranch and to Jed and, somehow, keep going.

"Miss Gold is a charming young creature," the madam—who had introduced herself as Mistress—was saying as they crossed the saloon. Matthew focused on keeping his stride even. He didn't want to betray a limp now. "I believe you will find her refined and talented. But of course," she went on, "we want you to be happy, so if there's anything else you require, please do not hesitate to let me know." Mistress turned her face up to Matthew and smiled.

She was a pretty lady, too—but there was something in that smile that made his skin crawl. He was a God-fearing man, although he had not been back to church since his Maria had died. This was a sin and he was probably going to hell, but then—wasn't he already in hell?

Before he could change his mind, they were in front of the girl in gold. Miss Gold. "Topaz, darling," Mistress said. "I would like you to meet Mr. Matthew Hawkins. He is visiting us from a ranch north of Decatur and I believe that you two would be well suited."

Matthew cringed. The woman made it sound like she was a matchmaker, not the proprietor of a whorehouse.

What was he doing here? He wasn't sure he could get his cock to respond if he wanted it to, so mortified he was. But just as he opened his mouth to excuse himself from the room—the building—Miss Topaz Gold looked up at him through thick lashes. There was something almost... innocent about her. She really was beautiful and she wasn't making eyes at him like some of the other ladies had done. He got the feeling she wasn't trying to seduce him and somehow, that made this okay. He didn't want to feel like a mark. He only wanted to feel like a man.

He whipped his hat off his head and held it in front of him. "Miss Gold, a pleasure to make your acquaintance."

She gave a little curtsy and his eyes followed her as her body dipped and raised. Compared to what he'd seen some of the other ladies in this building wearing, she was dressed almost appropriately—but there was no missing the creamy swell of her breasts as they surged above the bodice of her dress.

His cock stirred. Good. That was why he was here, wasn't it?

"Mr. Hawkins, I would be honored to spend an evening in your company." Her voice was low and had a husky quality to it that set his blood stirring a little faster. Maybe he could do this. Maybe he could enjoy himself. At the very least, maybe he could just stop thinking for one night.

Don't miss
HIS TOPAZ
By Maggie Chase
© 2017 by Maggie Chase

Check out www.maggiechase.com
for more great Jeweled Ladies stories!

Acknowledgements

I could not have written this book without the generous help of the following people: Melissa Jolly for everything she does, Amy Alessio for being awesome, Tasha Harrison and Liz Lincoln for editing, and Alexandra Haughton for designing the cover.

Dedication

To Liz Lincoln, who taught me the secret password to the Safehouse